FLIGHT

HUMANITY FOUND BOOK 2

PERRY WILSON

Ebook ISBN: 978-1-927669-72-3
Paperback ISBN: 978-1-927669-71-6
Audio book ISBN:978-1-927669-73-0

FREE EBOOK

Claim your copy of Running the Game when you use the QR code below to sign up for my newsletter and cheer on Pen as she vies for a commission in the military.

1

It's amazing what you can accomplish in three days, Pen thought as she entered the class of fifteen-year-olds to begin her first presentation. The students came from three different ships, some because their parents were transferred to *Dark Prospect* in a trade of skills, something that was impossible only a week ago. A few of the students came from Loke's ship; perhaps they would be looking at posting to other ships in the newly formed fleet. And of course, most were from *Dark Prospect* itself.

She hoped this wasn't a permanent assignment. Talking to civilians was a letdown. The battle to rescue the survivors of the final attack had been high stakes. The enemy had dogged them since as long as she could remember. Now they knew the truth and she wanted to keep solving big problems. Even her old duties seemed tame in comparison to the rescue, but Pen would happily go back to them to get away from school visits. When she'd tried to become one of the new type of scout, ones that flew patrols around *Dark Prospect*, she thought that would be perfect. Then the captain had called her and told her to come and talk to kids.

She scanned the faces while the teacher introduced her. A mix of boys and girls and maybe a few who weren't sure yet. At least no one was scowling at her; most had an expression of jaded boredom, like they'd heard it all. She ran her presentation through her mind. New info to them, but perhaps nothing to change the attitude of a normal teenager.

"I wonder what you've heard about the most recent events," Pen said. "Anyone want to volunteer?"

One girl looked around the room and then put her hand up slowly. Pen nodded at her.

She flicked her blond hair back and sat straight. "One of the ships was attacked and this time people escaped. A small team went to a planet and brought them back. And you brought back one of the enemy. And some of us were forced to move from our homes and come here."

"Pretty good summary. I'm sorry you had to change ships," Pen said. "What's your name?"

The girl looked at her neighbor and Pen saw her eyes roll. So, she'd managed to find allies. Maybe she would settle quickly. The girl turned back with a sigh.

"I'm Jarl."

"You transferred from *Joy Descending*?"

"My dad was traded for two of your communications officers. They made me come." Jarl crossed her arms and slumped back in her seat.

The captains of all the ships had made that decision. Pen was sure that the feelings of teenagers weren't part of the analysis. The ships needed to be united, and sharing expertise made that work. "You'll see your friends again," she said. "This is just temporary, until we are settled."

"Not for me." Another girl's hand shot up and she flicked a glance at Jarl as though apologizing for what she was about to say. She looked like a fashion model. Too much makeup for her age, pouty face, and well-coordinated clothes. She didn't need to flick her hair back. It was tightly woven into braids which highlighted her cheekbones as they twisted into a knot. "I'm Aila. I was on that planet."

"Then you probably know Loke," Pen said. "We met up with him when we came to find you."

"Yeah, well, he did his thing and now it's like our ship never existed. We don't have a home to go back to, so we should hang together, or our history will disappear."

"That won't happen, Aila." Pen tried to puzzle out the reason for the comments. So little time had passed since the rescue. How had these bad feelings gained so much strength? "You have your own leader. Loke will make sure your history is kept. When we find a home, we need all the history and experience we can get. Not just those who land, but all the knowledge held by the people who fought hard to keep us going so we could find a home."

"Yeah, that isn't likely to happen anytime soon," Jarl said.

The teacher stepped forward and clapped her hands. "Class, let's keep to the topic. Pen is here to answer your questions about the rescue, not to solve your problems."

It's not that clear cut. Pen felt naive for thinking the rescue was all a good thing. That coming together as a fleet would be seen as a step forward by everyone. She'd been preparing for the military all her life, so this moody teen stage had passed her by. Civilians didn't follow orders without question. The captains of each ship, or even one of them, should have known; should have found a way to spread the message as one of hope, not inconvenience.

"How much do you know about the enemy?" she asked. "We didn't only bring back the survivors of the attack. We learned something big."

Another girl's hand went up. This one had a sweet smile on her face, hair crimped so hard all evidence of the original tight curls gone except for a few rebellious twisted strands at her temples. "I'm Mellie. I grew up here. Tell us about the enemy. He's cute. But he killed so many of us. Can we trust him?"

Pen glanced around the room before answering. The boys watched the small group of girls who were monopolizing her time.

"Kalin's people believed us to be the enemy, as we were told his people were ours. He told me that our ships attacked them in the past. They lost everything too. There are people doing their best to figure out how we can trust him. But everyone on his ship was human. We need to find a way to work with them. We need all the humans we can find to make any settlement successful."

A chime sounded and every student suddenly shifted into gear, grabbing their devices and bags in their hurry to leave.

"Sorry about that," the teacher said. "This is rough for some of them. You did a good job."

That's a relief. "I'll let the captain know about the bad feelings. We should do more to help. Someone should be taking their side in the decisions and I don't think any of the civilian leaders are doing that."

OUTSIDE THE CLASSROOM, Pen turned to head for her duty station before remembering she was done for the day. What just happened didn't feel like a good job. Pen preferred the nice clean ending of most of her assignments. You achieved the goal, or you didn't. You succeeded or you failed. This was too much like failure and she couldn't see what success might look like.

She strode toward the dining hall. Maybe Jo would hear her out.

The captain needed to find someone qualified to be the spokesperson, she thought as she passed civilians in the corridor. Loke would be good at it, and he wasn't assigned anywhere yet. She would recommend him to the captain. Then she'd be available for a more interesting assignment.

As she ran through the list of people she knew, a lead ball formed in her stomach. She didn't need to tell the captain. He'd already chosen someone: her. This was her new assignment. It wasn't punishment; she'd done nothing wrong.

She stopped and found her way to the bulkhead. Leaning against the wall, she tried to understand why. Her future couldn't be made up of this gray feeling of ambiguous results. No. She would find a way to convince the captain that she made a better scout than a public relations hack. Scouts held lower rank, but a demotion was better than this.

"Pen?"

She looked up. Asher Jones was standing in front of her with a worried look on his face.

"Hi."

"I want to talk to you," he said. "Not here. My quarters; we'll have more privacy."

She remembered not trusting him at the beginning of the rescue mission. But he'd proved his worth and more at the end. "Sure. It's probably more interesting than what I planned to do." He was good at getting people to do things, so maybe she could ask him for advice about the captain.

Asher walked slightly ahead of her, using his height to subtly clear their path. Pen knew the schematics of the civilian part of the ship, but not the reality. On the military side, the corridors were crowded, but everyone was going somewhere with a purpose. Here, people clustered together and moved in groups, or blocked the way as they conducted a conversation. Having him lead meant she didn't get frustrated to the point of being rude.

His quarters were down a side corridor from the main one. The way was dimly lit, and the space narrow. Inside, his room looked much like hers: bed, desk, efficiency bathroom, chair.

In the chair was Roger Whitnal, the current civilian leader.

Pen turned to leave. "I have someplace to be."

"Wait," Asher said. "Just listen. I promise you will be interested, and we won't ask you to agree to anything."

She turned back. "Why is everything with you shady? You should have told me he would be here."

Whitnal stood and held out his hand, not to shake, but to offer the chair. "I don't understand why you feel this way about me, but I promise I'm not a bad man."

He was the reason Asher came with them on the mission. It worked out, but the man didn't know how to be straightforward with anyone.

"Okay," Pen said. She leaned against the wall next to the door. If they thought her stupid enough to sit where they could bar her exit, she'd show them how wrong they were.

Whitnal sat. He didn't look sneaky; short, balding and stocky, he looked like a kind grandfather. Looks could not be trusted.

"Okay, no preamble," Asher said. "We want you to join us."

"I'm military," she said. "I have no plans to change that."

"You helped me on the mission," Asher said. "I thought you might have the talents we need."

"Your captain doesn't seem to value your actual skill," Whitnal said. When Pen pushed from the wall to contradict him, he held up his hands in mock surrender. "Don't get me wrong. I admire the man. His job is hard. He's responsible for the safety of everyone on board -- on all the ships now. But I think he finds it hard to acknowledge the individual in all that."

"The captain knows what to do," Pen said. Well, maybe not this time, but she would find a way out of this assignment. "Why should I resign my commission? Something I've worked for all my life?"

Asher took a seat on the bed and waved Whitnal to silence.

Interesting. Who exactly is in charge here?

"People change, Pen," Asher said. "Things happen and people realize the life they built is fragile. Some change, some fight it; only the people who change survive."

In the short time since she'd come back from that planet, so much had changed. If she left the military there was no going back. It was too big a step.

"Just changing with the whims of the universe is weak," she said. "People have to control their fates."

"Fair enough," Whitnal said. "With all the new people aboard, and the other ships so close, I worry that we'll miss something important if we cling to the old ways. Promise me one thing."

"What?" No way was she going to promise anything blindly.

"Think it over." Whitnal rose. "I'll leave you to it."

He didn't even wait for her answer, just left her alone with Asher.

"Pen?" Asher said. "Will you?"

"Think it over? You mean, don't tell anyone, right?"

He nodded. "Until we know how this settles out, we can't trust anyone. I have a bad feeling about this exchange of people. I'm sure my counterparts on other ships sense it too."

"Yeah, people call it paranoia," she said. "What are you asking me to do? I can't promise to think over something I don't understand."

"Mostly we'll want you to listen and report on anything that doesn't feel right." He stared at her like her thoughts were running across her forehead. "You won't be interrogating anyone."

"No. You want me to send people to you so you can torture them."

"Not fair, Pen. We need to keep everyone safe too, and we don't torture people. We've taken an enemy aboard and let him roam free. You must see how that looks."

"Kalin wouldn't hurt anyone. His people abandoned him. We're his only choice."

"I hope so. Just consider it. And you can talk to your friends, but don't tell the captain. If you say no, then he won't ever learn we approached you. If you say yes, Roger will deal with it."

It felt like a betrayal, but she was going to say no, so it wouldn't be so bad. "Fine. I'll tell you my answer soon." She pulled open the door and slipped out before Asher could say anything more. His words were making too much sense for her to stay.

2

————

Too fast, Pen thought as she strode through the corridors away from Asher and his plans. Why is everything happening at once? She wanted to stop thinking over Asher's offer — she would not give any credit to Whitnal for it. The answer was no. If she hadn't agreed to keep the offer a secret from the captain, she could talk to Jo, but she couldn't be sure he would keep quiet. And she wouldn't go to him for answers. She might feel a trace of temptation, but she knew her answer.

The movement of the crowd became more purposeful, reminding Pen it was lunch time for her shift. Food would help. Her brain might be stuck on the offer because it needed sustenance.

She drifted with the stream of people headed for the dining hall. A week ago, the population of the ship was small enough that the military could have their own place to eat and relax. Now, with Loke's survivors and people from other ships, both halls were open to everyone, making for a noisier and more interesting mealtime.

She grabbed a tray and selected a roast vegetable sandwich and coffee before looking around for a table. Jocaster waved her to join him at one near the door.

"How did it go?" he asked.

"The class?" She unwrapped the sandwich and took a bite. It tasted of sweet vegetables fresh from the oven. The civilians got better cooks than the military.

"The whole morning. You did other things, right?" He handed his tray to a passing cleaning mech.

"Not much. The class only ended a while ago." *He can't know about Asher.*

He kept his gaze on the spoon he was using to stir his coffee. "Okay. How were the kids?"

"The teacher said I did okay," Pen said. "The kids hold all kinds of opinions on how the captain should run the ship."

He smiled up at her. "Didn't you at that age?"

"I focused on getting through the game," she said. They'd met when Jocaster pretended to be a contestant in the game that qualified winners to be officers. He was undercover, investigating the possibility it was fixed. "I guess I thought the captain knew what he was doing. Anyway, times are different now. We only had us, if you know what I mean."

"The new people came with different customs and beliefs," Jocaster said, nodding. "Less to question when we were kids."

She picked at her sandwich while she mulled that over. It was an opening. A way to talk to him about the choice she faced without spilling the facts. "Do you think we should have questioned things?"

"How?"

"Like just rebelled a bit," she said. She picked up her

sandwich and started to eat. If she had her mouth full, he'd have to talk.

"Before this, we were segregated. Civilians and military didn't cross much. Most kids who played the game came from military families, like me. I had no idea what the other kids thought. I had no frame of reference to question anything."

She took another bite and looked at him expectantly.

"Maybe we were odd, but I don't think so," he continued. "Maybe the civilian teenagers did rebel. But us, the people focused on a military career? We couldn't chance the blemish in our files."

The sandwich was gone, and Pen had nothing left to hide behind. "We survived, right? We were a healthy ship before this. If things were different, maybe Loke's people would be dead. We wouldn't know about Kalin's people."

"Yes," he said. "I'm not sure if it would have lasted that way. Yes, everything lined up to save the survivors. The fleet came together, and our captain is looking like a good leader."

"But?"

"If the civilians had more of a say, maybe we would be settled on a planet generations ago," Jo said, surprising her. "There would have been no war between Kalin's people and us. It's hard to know if our good outcome was the best we could do."

"True, but now things are going to change."

"Always do," he said. "Is that what you were talking to Asher about?"

So, he knew. Was he following her? "How do you know about that?"

"I saw him with you in the corridor." He shrugged. "You looked like you were heading somewhere."

"It was nothing," she said. At least he hadn't seen Whitnal. Jo wouldn't keep that quiet.

"He's bad news, Pen."

"He helped us on the mission," she said. "I agreed about him at the beginning, but he proved himself. You should give him a break."

"He's a bit old for you."

"More than a bit."

"Not a date then." He wouldn't meet her eyes.

She tried for casual and stuffed her annoyance down where it wouldn't start a confrontation. "No, and why are you so curious? I'm allowed a private life."

"Nothing on the ship is really private, Pen. I think you should stay away from him regardless of why you went with him. How will it look to the captain?"

Why should she care what people thought? The captain knew her and if he didn't, it was too late. This morning was stacking up to be a horrible day; spoiled kids, spies, and now Jo acting the big brother. "I can look after my own reputation, thanks." She crumpled the sandwich wrapper into a ball and tossed it into her empty cup. A cleaning mech approached and slid out a grabber to take the trash to be recycled. Her bad temper wasn't that easy to shake.

"We're under more scrutiny," Jo said. "The rescue put us in the spotlight. The captain is watching us more than usual."

"Look, Jo," she said, standing and trying not to shout. "I can take care of myself. I'm not stupid and I get to do things with other people, not just you."

Now he looked like he was getting ready to apologize, but Pen didn't want to hear it.

"No, don't bother. I can look after myself, Jo. You are not my superior, or my mentor. I thought you were my friend, but..." The next words would be hard to take back if she let them out.

"I am."

"Okay, then be the friend who gives me a bit of room to breathe."

3

"You look like you need a referee." Loke put his tray down and slipped into the remaining chair. "What's going on?"

Part of her wanted to leave, but maybe he could be an ally. The only history they had was the successful rescue.

"It's not that bad," she said, unwilling to admit even to herself how close she'd come to running away. "How are things settling for your people?"

"Hard to say. There are so many new people aboard, we kind of blend in." He poked at his plate of hash. "I think maybe the people who've been here the longest are in shock. Finding out that the enemy was just us, and taking in the survivors, and trading experts between ships; a lot to digest."

"It'll take a while," Jo said. "And two more ships are arriving in the next twelve hours. There's no time to absorb the changes."

The noise in the dining hall rose as it filled with people. Pen kept her voice low to avoid attracting attention. "If you stop to deal with your feelings, ten other changes will happen, and you'll fall further behind."

Jo shook his head like she was missing the point. "I meant things will keep changing. Accept and move on, that's my way."

This wasn't the argument she expected. Pen kept quiet.

"Of course, if you don't stand still for a bit, you never get ahead." Jo looked at Loke. "Pen's thinking of leaving the military."

He beat her to it. If Loke took Jo's side... She let the thought go; it didn't matter now.

"That's what you were fighting about?" Loke laughed. "With everything going on, seems a bit petty."

"Not to me," Pen said. "It's my future. Jo thinks we'll stop being friends if I'm not part of the military. That's not true, right?"

Loke shrugged and kept eating.

"It has to be," Jo said. "We won't see each other as much. We'll both know things we can't discuss. You'll make other friends."

"That's just old thinking," Pen said. If Loke wasn't going to help, she'd keep trying to make Jo understand. He meant so much to her, but not enough to risk the rest of her life on. "We kept separate, the civilians and the military. Now, that will change. The enemy is gone; we need to start building relationships that will help create a new home when we find a planet."

"You don't know that," Jo said. "Who's going to find the new world? Us. The military. Who's going to manage the creation of a colony? Us again. The civilians don't have the skills."

Pen hadn't thought about that. Was Jo right? She'd thought the future would open up the boundaries between the two groups. That living on a planet would mean they had to work together.

"Loke, you come from a different culture," she said. "Were your experts all military?"

He looked at his plate like he wanted to avoid answering, but it was empty. "It's not that straightforward. All of us were trained to fight. There wasn't a civilian side, more like a reserve military. Your ship is probably the only one with enough people to do that. But our way didn't guarantee safety. If it did, we would still have a ship."

"Same on Kalin's ship," Jo said. "They didn't allow any passengers."

"Don't call them that," Pen said. She hated the way the military dismissed the civilians. "Whatever we did in the past will have to change. We've traded military experts for civilian ones from the other ships. It must change."

"But you don't have to be one to take the first step," Jo said. "Wait until things settle down. Then you can decide."

"When things settle down, the opportunities will be gone." Why couldn't he be happy for her? Why didn't Loke take her side?

"And there will be more opportunities in the military," Jo argued. "Why do you have to leave?"

Why did he have to ask a good question? Pen thought about her answer, trying to think through her anger for a rational reason. "I think because no one else is offering."

"What do you mean?" Loke asked. "The captain must be giving you some reward for the rescue."

Pen slumped back in her chair. "Not really," she said. "Jo, what is your new assignment?"

"A bunch of training. I'm working with the engineers first. Next, the scouts I think."

"Sounds like you're in for an interesting future," Loke said. "What are you doing, Pen?"

"Talking to teenagers." Pen tried to keep the resentment out of her voice. It didn't work. "That's what the captain thinks of me."

"You can't be sure what he thinks of you," Jo said. "He could have big plans."

"I doubt it," Pen said. "He always saw you as the star. I told you that on the planet. I get all the blame. He's pushing me into a dead end."

These thoughts were new. They must have been in the back of her mind, but looking them over, she realized how much of a betrayal it felt. This conversation was only going to end in yelling and crying. "I'll see you later."

She slipped out the door and ran to the next turn in the corridor, looking for somewhere to calm down privately. She hated fighting with Jo. And this incident proved it wasn't about taking a job; it was about leaving one.

4

More people filled the corridor than Pen expected. She wanted a quiet place to sort out everything whirling around in her brain. The observation lounge would be a great place. Staring out into space and stars wouldn't get in the way of thinking.

"Oh, hi."

A voice broke through her concentration. It was one of the girls from this morning. Four of them were clustered together staring at her. She had no idea which one had spoken.

"Yeah, hi. Are you finished for the day?" It was lame, but she couldn't think of anything else.

"Just for lunch," Mellie said. One of the girls from *Dark Prospect*. "We didn't expect you to be hanging around the civilian halls."

These girls were like Jo. They held on to the old ways. "It's open to all now," Pen said. "Are you looking for someone?" Maybe she could point them on their way.

"No, but since you are here," Mellie said, "we wanted to talk to you anyway."

The four girls moved toward her, backing Pen against the bulkhead to avoid physical contact. Everything about them screamed power play.

It was odd to see such different girls acting like a gang. Mellie and Aila, both dressed and made up like popular girls, all gloss and attitude. The other two, Jarl and Flor, didn't belong with them. Jarl looked like an athlete and Flor like a tech student. This group of girls showed the best example of how much the world had changed. If Jocaster cared to look, he wouldn't argue about how different things were now.

She stepped forward so they had to retreat. She would not cede the power position. "What can I help with?"

"You can talk to the captain, right?" Jarl said. "You can tell him we want to go back to our ships."

"Your ships? I thought you were the only transfer family. Aila, you don't have a ship to go back to." Not exactly diplomatic, but she didn't have the patience for it.

Aila tipped her head as though thinking about what Pen said. "We don't all want to stay here. Other ships are more... suitable."

"What do your parents think? If they are unhappy, I'm sure the captain will listen."

Jarl sniffed. "My dad doesn't care. He just looks at the work he's been given and doesn't even see how it affects me."

There was no way Pen would waste the captain's time with petty teenage moaning. They were always unhappy. She remembered being easy to upset at that age, but she'd had her eyes firmly set on the military, so she'd kept her emotions under control. She'd had fewer choices at that age than these girls, too.

"What's so bad about being here? We'll find a planet soon, I'm sure. All the ships will come together."

"Sure. We've all heard that since we were kids." Mellie smirked. "We're not that gullible. I've lost friends to other ships. Jarl misses her team, Aila doesn't like the way the military looks down on the civilians. Flor's boyfriend got sent to Jarl's ship. We shouldn't be forced to give things up."

Pen sympathized a little. But at that age all her friends were headed for the game and an officer's rank. She couldn't really relate but believed it would get better for them. But if they didn't lose the selfish act, they'd end up lonely. Even civilians knew it was important to work together and make sacrifices.

"Jarl, what did you play on your ship?"

"I was head of the flash hockey team." Her voice carried some pride.

"We have teams on this ship," she said. "Jarl, you'll find a place."

"The teams are all full. No one will add me now. And if they did, I wouldn't be in the head position." Jarl actually sounded hurt.

"Did the coach tell you that?" Pen could talk to the captain if that was the case. Everyone needed to accommodate a few things to help integrate the new people.

"I didn't bother trying out. I know how it works."

This wasn't the place to deal with their problems. Pen was sure she wasn't the person to help either, but at least she could give them a few ideas. "It sounds like you have a lot of problems to deal with," she said. "The ship's counselors will know how to help."

"We don't need that kind of help. We know what we want, and we thought you would care." Mellie turned to the others. "Let's go, she's useless."

"Wait," Pen said. She couldn't let them go. Being annoying was hardly a reason to let someone hurt the way these girls were hurting. "Give it a chance. You've already made friends. If you still feel like this in a few weeks, tell your teacher. She has access to resources for her students."

"Like I said, useless," Mellie said and then took the group toward the dining hall.

Pen watched them leave and then headed for the observation lounge. This interaction was a great example of why she was not cut out for this role.

5

The observation room was usually empty; most people were too busy with their lives to spend time staring at screens. The scenery didn't change fast enough to be interesting and people could find better meditation environments elsewhere.

The far wall was a bank of what looked like windows but were really screens. They displayed the feed from outside sensors. For a while the scouts sent feeds from their ships, but it was too dizzying and now all she saw were stars that looked set in place, and black between them.

She moved to one of the couches placed for observation before noticing she wasn't alone. Kalin was curled up staring out at the view a couple of couches away. Pen walked over, hoping he would be willing to talk. He might understand her problem, and since his people had abandoned him, he had to figure out his place in the new ship from the beginning. Many people still saw him as an enemy and she didn't know how he coped.

"Hi," she said quietly. "Are you okay?"

He turned his gaze from the screens to her. He looked exhausted. "I don't need help."

"How long have you been here?" Suddenly her problems seemed much too small to ask for his assistance. "Won't someone miss you?"

He stretched and then patted the couch. "Who would do that? I have no friends here."

Pen ignored his words and followed his invitation to sit. "Hasn't the captain given you a guide? You need one just to get around and help you figure out what you can do."

"Who would trust me?" He looked at the screen again. "I want to see my ship before anyone else. If they are waiting for me, I have to decide what to do."

"What do you mean? Won't you explain that we aren't the enemy? Your people need us."

He nodded and turned to her. "It will not be easy. I've seen what you are. I know if we don't join the fleet, we will die out; we are too few to survive."

Pen waited. She wanted to let him get through whatever was worrying him. He needed a counselor, but she figured he wasn't ready to hear that.

"I believe we should change, but I don't think we can. It has been the same on my ship since I can remember. How will I convince them?"

"You'll think of something," she said. "If you can't make them understand, what will you do? You can stay here."

"This is not my home." He slid a little closer to the arm of the couch, creating more distance between them.

"It could be." Pen thought about the girls. Their problem was insignificant in the scheme of things, but the pain was the same. Maybe Kalin should know that he wasn't alone. Would telling him violate some kind of privacy agreement?

She decided to wait until later. Kalin needed her attention even if he didn't think he wanted it.

He looked at his clenched hands. "It is not that easy. I must choose between a dying culture and a place where I will always have to live with the knowledge that most people are just waiting for me to turn into a killer. Loke's people look at me and I see every one of their friends and family that I killed."

"That's not what they think," Pen said. Her immediate reaction didn't ring true in her own ears. If she'd come from Loke's ship she would always think of the dead when she looked at Kalin. "Have you talked to a counselor? No matter whether you choose to go or stay, you need help."

"I will deal with my problems myself." He turned back to the screens. "It may not be my choice. They abandoned me once, perhaps I will not be welcomed back. Or perhaps I will be and then executed."

Her problems fizzled out in the face of Kalin's. No matter what Pen chose, eventually things would work out. All Kalin saw was darkness in his future. "Maybe you won't have to face it. If we don't find the ship soon, we'll stop looking."

"And I will be stuck here."

That was not what she wanted him to take from her statement, but Pen realized she didn't have the skills to help him. All she could do was keep trying to make a connection with the man behind the pain. She didn't see a killer when she looked at him. Even though he would have slaughtered them if his mission had been successful, he was a product of his training. He would eventually understand that the world was not full of enemies. When he did, she would be there to prove she was a friend. "I'll watch with you for a while," she said, curling up into the corner of the couch.

"I would prefer to be alone."

She stood. "Okay. Please remember we aren't your adversary, and you aren't our enemy now."

SHE APPRECIATED the light duties today; with no need to report to anyone, she had the time to think things through. A coffee and a quiet table were exactly what she needed. The dining hall was fairly empty when she returned to it.

Pen chose a seat in the corner, placed her coffee and pad on the table and tried to order her thoughts. The more time that passed since meeting with Asher, the more complicated the decision became. And now she had Kalin's problems to deal with. It was hard to keep focused on one thing when everything felt urgent.

"I need to apologize." Jo's voice broke the chaos of her thoughts.

He stood with a coffee in one hand and a plate of pastries in the other. He waited for her nod before sitting.

"I guess we kind of lost it," Pen said. "Can we start again?"

"Wait. You didn't give me a chance to say sorry yet." He grinned and pushed the pastries toward her. "This is a bribe in case you missed the point. I shouldn't have reacted that way. It wasn't about you doing something different. I don't want to lose you; you are my best friend." He grinned at her. "How was that?"

"Who told you to say those words?" Pen knew Jo wouldn't have said the best friend thing without prompting.

"Loke," Jo said. "Did it work?"

Pen looked around and noticed Loke hanging out near the door. She waved him over. "Yes. I'm still deciding about the offer. Maybe we can talk it through?" *Why did I say that? I am going to say no.*

Loke glanced at her pad. "You've got quite a list."

"Not just my problems," she said. Maybe Loke could tell if his group of survivors really believed Kalin would always be a killer. "Kalin is in bad shape."

"Let him figure it out," Jo said. "You have no idea what he's going through. No one does."

"I'm afraid he'll make a bad decision," Pen said. She kept Kalin's feelings to herself but that didn't mean she couldn't do a little research. "Will your people ever accept him?" she asked Loke.

"We aren't all the same," Loke said. "There will always be some who can't put the past where it belongs."

"It's not like we're angels," Jo said. "We would have blown his ship out of the sky if we could."

"Yes, but you didn't," Kalin said, sliding onto the empty stool.

He'd come on them while Pen was concentrating on Loke's words.

She smiled to welcome him and maybe show a bit more empathy. "We really are trying to help."

"You can't help me," he said, but he stayed anyway. "You haven't ever boarded a ship and killed everyone. How can you know what I feel?"

"You aren't the only one who has problems," Loke said. "How about you try helping Pen?"

Kalin glared at him.

"You don't have to," she said. "I can work out my own issues."

It looked for a minute like he was going to leave. Instead of helping, she'd made things worse. Pen tried to pull her words together to make him stay. Before she could speak, Kalin relaxed.

"Okay, what's the big problem?" he asked. "It will be nice to think about something else for a while."

Pen told them about Asher's offer, leaving out Whitnal's contribution. If she did this it would be because of Asher, not because of some political sleaze. She noticed Jo working hard to keep his face neutral.

"Why are you having difficulties?" Kalin asked. "Who is the superior officer? You should bow to their orders."

"Wow, you are different," Loke said. "Even I can tell this ship is divided sharply between the civilians and the military."

Jo took a sip of his coffee, still controlling his reaction. "I guess no one has given you an orientation," he said. "The captain is in charge of the protection of the ship and finding a home planet... I guess now that's all the captains. The civilian leader, Whitnal, is in charge of making sure the community is strong enough to colonize when we land."

"So, you have a real choice?" Kalin seemed completely shocked. "If you are able to make such decisions, how is this ship not in chaos?"

Today it felt to Pen like it already was. "Mostly we follow orders. The military is led by the captain, so I follow his orders."

"What does he think about this?" Kalin asked. "On my ship, I would not have to ask that question. Here, you have looser rules. You talk to your captain, right?"

It didn't feel like she was ready to talk to the captain about anything. Pen realized she'd lost her unquestioned trust in him. He'd assigned her to this stupid school thing, after all. If he expected her to see that as a reward, she didn't know him as well as she thought.

"Most times," Pen said.

"It would be good to do that," Jo said. "Maybe he has a plan for you."

"I'm tired of trying to figure out his plan," Pen said. "I guess that's the biggest reason I didn't tell Asher no." Well, she had, but here she was still thinking about his offer.

"It's a big decision," Loke said. "If you want out of the military, you might have other options."

"I am not going to leave the military." Pen stopped herself from banging her fist on the table in frustration.

"I don't understand how you get through the day," Kalin said. "But you were right. My problems don't seem so big now. They are mostly behind me, after all."

Pen watched the four girls slip in through the door and head for the counter. Maybe she should ask Kalin to talk to them. Maybe, but not yet.

"She doesn't want out," Jo said.

Pen watched the girls. Their dissatisfaction didn't show even if you knew it was there.

"How do you know that?" Kalin asked.

"Pen has been aiming for this since she was a kid. You don't just get handed a commission."

She kept her attention split between the conversation that seemed to be going on without her input, and the girls who were now huddled around a table. Maybe the choices weren't just taking or not taking Asher's offer. Despite resisting involvement, Pen couldn't stop worrying about the four girls, and who knew how many more felt the same way but didn't speak.

"Asher seemed like a good guy," Loke said.

"He could have been a lot worse with me," Kalin added.

"He's still capable of some pretty awful things," Jo said.

What about being a counselor, or a teacher? No, not

teacher; no more teenage angst, but she could be trained on almost any other job.

"But you don't know if he's actually done anything." Loke had taken on the role of Asher's defender.

With the right training, she could help people like Kalin too. He couldn't be the only one feeling lost.

"I know what he told me he did." Jo poked her. "Have you lost interest? These are your problems."

She let the girls go; they weren't currently upset, and she wasn't an expert at the job, but she knew to let well enough alone.

"You seem to be capable of hashing it out without me." She laughed as he started to apologize. "Just kidding. I don't think we're going to figure this out easily. Talking helped, thanks."

"And me," Kalin said. "I will think about taking charge of my life. I don't hold out much hope, but it's better than moping."

"I think I need more information," Pen said. "I won't announce any decision without telling you first."

She wasn't lying. Just this short time of not fighting about it gave her perspective. No one could force her to decide before she was ready.

Loke nodded to Kalin. "Maybe come talk to my family and some of my friends."

Kalin drew away. "I can't."

"Okay. When you're ready. I promise not everyone hates you."

The cross-ship announcement chimed before Kalin could respond. *Lieutenants Tromarin and Bryman, report to the captain's quarters. Civilian Kalin, your presence is requested.*

Pen looked at Jo. "I didn't do anything wrong." The captain couldn't know about Asher and Whitnal yet. "And he wouldn't call Kalin along if we were in for a dressing down."

A young girl ran up to Loke. "They are looking for you. You need to go to the captain." She ran away without waiting for Loke to respond.

"Why do you get a private invitation?" Pen asked.

"They seem to think we should be treated specially. It's like we are our own ship within your ship. Probably not great for integration."

"We shouldn't keep him waiting," Jo said. "If it involves all of us, perhaps Pen is right and she's not about to get in trouble for something."

Pen threw up her hands. "I'm not always getting into trouble."

6

Despite her words, Pen ran the last few days through her mind as they hurried to the captain's quarters. The only thing that stood out was the class. Had the teacher complained? Or one of the parents? She hadn't really done anything wrong. If her performance wasn't up to expectations, there was hope for a new assignment.

The captain was alone in his quarters, but two marines stood outside. It was unusual for him to need a guard; Pen wondered why they were there.

"Thank you for coming," he said. "I need you to agree to keep what you are about to learn to yourselves until the official announcement."

"Jo and I will follow your orders," Pen said.

Loke looked at Kalin; both men seemed puzzled.

Kalin spoke first. "If it will not do harm, I will keep your secret."

"Like he said," Loke added. "I'm not keeping secrets that will hurt my people."

Pen waited for the captain to dismiss them. No one added caveats to his orders.

"It will do no harm to keep the secret for a few hours," he said. "I cannot say how much harm will come after we announce. I am telling you four now in hopes that you will work to contain any reactions."

He wouldn't do that if the news was good. Pen didn't want to hear any more bad news. But it wasn't up to her.

"I guess we can agree to that," Loke said, checking with Kalin who nodded.

"Thank you," the captain said without a trace of sarcasm. Pen wondered if he was so diplomatic to all civilians. He could simply put them in the brig for the time he needed before announcing.

"We found Kalin's ship."

Relief and fear vibrated through Pen. Would Kalin join them? Were they headed for a battle?

"Have you contacted them?" Kalin stepped forward. "I can give you the protocols. Perhaps I should be the one who reaches out."

The captain held up his hand. "It is not what we hoped. Something has destroyed the ship. I'm sorry, Kalin. There is nothing but scraps left."

Pen reached for Kalin's arm. He pulled away and looked around the small room like he needed to escape. Then he froze, fists clenched, stare locked on a blank wall.

"Show me," he finally said.

"Of course." The captain tapped his pad and the image of space popped up on the wall.

The black was scattered with ship pieces. With nothing to compare to, the pieces looked small enough to hold in her hand. Pen knew the false perspective tricked her eye. One of the closest shards was a hatch; it would be larger than the observation room.

"No bodies?" Kalin asked. "How are there no bodies?"

"Scouts are approaching the wreckage. One of the reasons we want to hold back on announcing. We don't know if it's a rescue mission yet."

"What do you want from us?" Jo asked.

"Two things. I wanted to give Kalin time to recover from the shock." He turned to face Kalin. "It will take more than a few hours for you to deal with this, but it wouldn't be fair to drop this on you at the same time as everyone else."

"How can I be sure you didn't do this?" Kalin asked, his voice tight.

Pen wouldn't let him turn his shock into anger. "If we had this power, your ships would never have taken us. Is this something your ships could do?"

"Maybe you developed it recently. Our ships have disappeared over the years. This must be why. I want to go with the scouts."

"They already left," the captain said. "I sent them all in case we needed to bring back anyone who escaped. You can watch the feed from their probes here. I will answer any questions you want."

"You wanted us here for more than just this," Loke said.

"This discovery changes our future," the captain said. "We did not do this. Kalin's ship was the only one of their kind left. It means we have a real alien enemy."

Pen looked at the projection again. This was a fight they couldn't win. But how could they run? "If the people who did this are still near, we are in danger."

"One of the reasons all the scouts are out. If the perpetrator is still in the vicinity, we need to know. They are also gathering as much information from the debris as they can.

We may be forced to fight and right now, we don't have much chance."

"If we lose all the scouts, we can't keep watch," Jo said.

"You understand," the captain said. "I will be talking to the other captains and my executive officers. Whitnal and other civilians will be involved. I need to talk to you. You've formed a bond, and Kalin might know information we don't. That means you might see a different perspective."

"Whatever happens," Kalin said, "I will eventually get revenge. Not today, but I will not rest until I have shown them the error of attacking my people."

"We have the whole fleet to worry about, young man, but I understand, and I hope you will be successful. There was no need for such wanton destruction."

"The scouts passed through the outer debris field," Pen said. "Oh, Kalin, I'm so sorry."

The first feeds showed the fate of the people on Kalin's ship. Bright mists of organic material, each emanating from an environmental suit.

7

The scouts were still searching the wreckage when Pen convinced Kalin to leave. They found a place in the dining hall that was filling with people in preparation for the announcement. It was scheduled to happen in only a half hour. The crowd looked curious, and a few people turned their way, clearly wondering if the summons earlier was connected. No one asked questions.

"How are we going to fight something like that?" Loke asked quietly. "What plans could be coming so soon after the discovery?"

Pen wished she had the answer. Kalin was too shocked to offer suggestions when the captain asked. The only thing any of them offered was to find a way to conceal the fleet before heading for a fight. If this ship-killer was gone, it would take time to find them. Training more fighters was possible; training more scouts and converting shuttles to reinforce the defense capability not as easy. Knowing about the danger had to make a difference if the attackers showed up.

Eventually the captain had given up asking and just let

them observe the feeds. The bodies were clustered as if arranged there; hundreds of them. The debris spread out from there in a sphere. Pen tried to picture the attack. The only way she could visualize it was some weapon passing through the shielding and blowing up the power core. That would mean all the people on the ship huddled at the center, or someone had taken them prisoner, herded them together and then killed them.

"Are you sure there are no survivors?" she asked Kalin. "The number of..." She couldn't quite finish the sentence.

"Bodies?" he snapped. "You don't have to protect me. I'm a soldier, remember? And they left me to die at your hands. They weren't my people anymore."

The words were so different from his earlier hope that they would take him back. "You still knew them."

Loke elbowed her to stop and leaned in. "You aren't the only one who lost people. Don't pretend you aren't hurting, soldier. Are there enough bodies to account for the whole ship complement?"

Kalin straightened. "If they took prisoners, it was only one or two. Will the scouts report the actual numbers?"

"Yes," Jo said. "But we need to know if we should be thinking about rescue."

"Revenge," Kalin said. "We kill our enemies."

The conversation ended as the call for attention went out. After a few moments to allow the audience to focus, the captain started speaking.

He began with reminding people of the fleet's primary goal: to find a new planet where humanity could start again and be safe. The crowd murmured agreement.

For the last three days, our immediate goal has been to find our former enemy's ship. Our intention was to invite them to join the fleet; all humans are welcome in the search for a new home.

Almost half the audience turned to look at Kalin. Not all of them with resentment.

We found them, and someone or something destroyed the ship and its crew. The feeds will be updated by the time this announcement is over; please be aware the images are graphic and disturbing.

The expression on people's faces changed as they turned to look at Kalin again. Now it was sympathy on most, and a sick gloating on a few. Only the knowledge no ship in the fleet had the capability of that level of destruction kept Pen from suspecting the attack came from her ship.

As you will see, we do not currently have the capability to fight such a force. With that in mind, we believe engaging is not the best action. Whatever did this is not in the area; we have time.

Now the muttering had an edge. Pen felt Jo tense beside her. Loke wasn't yet aware of the shift, or if he was, he kept his reaction hidden. Kalin worried her. He glared back at the people who looked their way. She touched his arm. He turned to her, eyes narrowed.

"Stay calm," she said. "Remember, this is the first time they've heard this. They don't want a fight." She hoped showing Kalin was part of the team would soften the anger in him, and in the watchers.

"I will not start a fight," Kalin said.

The unspoken *I will finish one* worried Pen more than his outward aggression.

The announcement continued. *After consulting with all the leaders in the fleet, we reached a decision on our strategy. We will wait here, gathering intelligence from the wreckage, until all ships have joined us. The scouts will continue to patrol at the edges of our sensor range for any sign of the real enemy. When we are together, we will leave to find our new home.*

Pen could see people talking, but no sound penetrated

her shock. They were leaving as soon as they could? Not even making preparations to go after the killers? Sound came back as she struggled to answer her own questions.

The announcement closed with a reminder that people could watch the feeds if they desired and a promise of more information when it became available.

Pen struggled with an urge to control the crowd. People needed space to think and she'd be as likely to start a riot as calm them. She focused on trying to hear what was being said. Loke and Jo seemed to be doing the same. Only Kalin ignored the voices.

"It's going to be fine," Jo said. "Most of the people here agree with the decision, right?"

"It is what they are saying," Loke said. "What happens for the people who don't?"

"Probably an open session with some of the spokespeople. The captain will allow dissent, but he has made a decision and it won't change."

Pen waited for Jo to continue, to tell them what he thought, but he didn't. "Do you agree?" she asked.

"People with the right level of authority made the decision," Jo said. "It doesn't matter what I think. We will receive our orders."

Kalin was still withdrawn so Pen looked to Loke for help. He watched as the room emptied.

"They are going to look at the carnage," Loke said. "Do you think it will change minds?"

"To what?" Kalin asked. "Your captain is right. Even if he is not, you must obey your orders, like Jocaster said. You think I didn't want to question my superiors? I did, but it was their job to make decisions and mine to act on the orders."

"And look how well that turned out," Pen said, regretting it the moment the words came out.

"How good was your ship at defense?" Loke asked. "I mean, how did they get surprised? You noticed we found no evidence they fought back, right?"

"There is always an enemy you cannot defend against. For generations, we thought the only one we had was you. We lost so many ships and the only cause had to be your fleet. That is why we started to attack. It was self-defense at first." He closed his eyes. "I am surprised they didn't have time to fight back. We were always on alert."

"So how will we be sure they aren't just dogging us?" Loke nodded toward the last of the audience drifting out of the room. "The question will come as soon as they see what happened."

Pen realized she'd taken the captain at his word that the scouts could tell if the killer lurked nearby. "At least we gathered data from the remains of the ship," she said. "I'm not saying it means we should run, but it is a bit of assurance that we can."

"This isn't like you, Pen." Jo shook his head. "I mean, you never questioned decisions before. You were always up for fun, but never to outright disobey."

"Before we went on the mission," she said. "Jo, running isn't going to make us safe. If the ship-killer wants us, they will find us. Being on a planet won't make us any safer."

"She's right," Loke said. "We have to eliminate this threat before we settle."

"There will be other threats," Kalin said.

"And we'll fight them too," Loke said.

"How?" Jo waved his hand between them to stop the argument gaining momentum. "How would you fight something like this? We have no weapons strong enough, and we have no defenses against them."

"We don't know about the weapons," Pen said. "We will find out about shielding when all the data is in. I am sure of it."

"Then talk to the captain," Jo said. "Wait until the data is in. If it shows anything we can use, talk to him. Or you can just accept Asher's offer. As a civilian you can question anything you want." He stood and marched out of the room.

Pen let him go. She needed more information before she did anything. It hurt that he couldn't or wouldn't take her side. She hadn't had a chance to say she knew a real right answer didn't exist. But she was as worried as Loke that they couldn't avoid a meeting with whoever destroyed Kalin's ship.

"Kalin, you will be asked to help with the analysis," she said. "Only you know what data applies to your ship and what might be the aliens." She hoped they were aliens. If this turned out to be another group of humans, how could anyone feel safe, ever?

"I will help," he said. "The captain only needs to order me."

"Did you really believe we were capable of that?" Loke asked. "When you saw it, you thought we did it."

"I didn't think. You have been the adversary for so long I simply reacted. But no. If you had that capability, I wouldn't be here to help." He pushed away from the table and left Pen and Loke alone.

8

"I can't sit here worrying," Pen said. "I'll see you later."

Loke followed her to the hall. "I need to go talk to my family."

Pen watched him walk away and then decided to go to her own quarters. She would be able to think in the quiet room and watch the feeds at the same time. If there was hope in the information, she wanted to find it right away.

"Lieutenant Tromarin?"

Pen looked up; Mellie stood blocking her way. Her three cohorts ranged behind, arms crossed. They looked ridiculous; Pen considered walking through what they thought was probably a barrier but decided now wasn't the time to antagonize anyone, so she would let them have their moment. She didn't want to deal with their petty problems; didn't they realize the danger the whole fleet was in?

"Yes?" Pen said. She didn't need to be anything more than civil. The faster they got through what they wanted to say, the faster she'd get time to think.

"Did the captain even think we had an opinion?" Mellie

looked back at her friends. Pen watched them nod encouragement. "He just made a decision that affected all of us."

"It is his job," Pen said. "I'm sure he asked for advice from the other captains. And the civilian leaders too."

"But did he listen to them?" Mellie asked. "He should have asked us to vote on the plan."

Pen tried not to judge the whine in her voice. Even if she didn't agree with the decision, she wasn't naive enough to think allowing votes on vital decisions would ever work. "It's the captain's job to decide what is best for the ship, and now the fleet. You don't have enough information to cast an informed vote."

"That's the problem," Mellie said. Jarl muttered something in agreement.

"No. It's not a problem," Pen said. "Maybe someday we will be in a safe place where everyone gets a voice. But right now, we are in space and we've just encountered a threat that could end humanity. There's no time for debating; no time for mistakes."

"I thought you might have the guts to tell the captain what we thought," Mellie said. "But you're clearly a lackey. We won't waste any more of our time with you. I'm sure we can find someone who will help."

She moved to step past Pen.

"Wait," Pen said, reaching for Mellie's arm. "Don't do anything to get yourselves in trouble. I know you think this is unfair, but if you start questioning things the wrong way, you'll be put in the brig."

"My parents wouldn't allow it."

"We are at war." Pen looked all the girls in the eye. "That means we can't afford distractions. Your parents won't be able to save you if someone reports you are trying to rebel. And someone will."

Mellie looked at Pen's hand. "Let me go."

"Did you hear me?"

"Yes. Are you going to report us?"

Pen wondered if she should. Right now, they were only scared kids. Perhaps if she gave them time and a way forward it would be okay. It didn't help that she agreed with them about the plan not feeling like the best choice. She would follow orders regardless.

"No. You can talk to your teacher, or your parents. They will know the best way for you to express your opinion without getting into trouble you don't want."

"Fine." Mellie turned to the others. "Let's go."

Pen stood aside, giving them the illusion of winning. She needed privacy more than ever now.

FINALLY IN HER QUARTERS, Pen locked the door and called up the feeds. She sat at her desk and tried to assimilate the avalanche of information. The scouts had tested each of the clusters. Since the captain had sent all of the ships, it didn't take long to get whatever they needed. Each blood sample tested out to different individuals. All related, which was not a surprise after being in a closed system for so long.

So, there were far fewer of the enemy than expected, and Kalin could tell them if the list was complete. The facts didn't help her work out her feelings; she'd known they died, and they were strangers, but she still felt loss. She flipped the view to the tests on the physical objects. The metals and electronics that survived.

Burns scored the larger pieces on what would have been the inside of the ship. Was it possible the core breached, and no attack happened? It was hard to believe Kalin's people would have been negligent. Cores were built to last; no other ship had been lost that way — unless it was only the start. Too many questions; she would need to wait for the conclusions. Analysis experts could confirm or exclude a breach.

Someone was already broadcasting simulations—official ones, so they were reliable, not biased to make a point. Two in particular drew her attention. The first showed what the data supported. The video started with a ship in space, one that looked much like Dark Prospect, then it exploded slowly like some giant flower opening. The result was the pattern the scouts had found. The only disparity was the bodies; in the simulation they floated scattered throughout the debris, not arranged together.

The second simulation kept running the explosion. This one focused on the location of the slaughtered crew. Each time it iterated, the screen flickered and then the cycle started again. Pen leaned in closer and stared. Each time the screen flickered, data points turned red. They didn't fit the results. The computer was trying to find a scenario where the placement of the bodies could be explained. Or, explained without the assumption they'd been arranged. It wasn't working. So, not a core breach.

Someone knocked.

She activated the door scanner. If it was anyone trying to argue her around to their point of view, she'd ignore them. Before she took a side, she needed to be clear on her own thoughts.

Asher!

Pen released the lock. He would have a different take on this and she didn't need to agree or disagree with him.

"I've been looking for you," he said as he stepped into her quarters. "I didn't expect you to be home at this time."

"Okay. Why?" Pen turned off the feed.

"Things have changed." He looked around for another

chair, but Pen's quarters were standard. If he wanted a seat, he could perch on the bed. He looked reluctant but folded himself to do just that. The bed was low, and it put him in an awkward position.

"No kidding. I'm not sure why you think I can do anything about it."

"You saw the most recent data?"

"Yes." If he thought she was going to offer more than simple answers, he would be disappointed.

"It's more important now to get the right people in the right roles."

The job offer had faded into the background of her thoughts. "No. I'm not leaving the captain. I'm not spying on him."

"Did you talk to him about it?" Asher showed no inclination to accept her answer.

That wouldn't be a good idea, Pen thought. "No need to. I'm not helping you."

"You should talk to him."

The conversation wasn't going anywhere. Pen decided to try getting some information from Asher. "So, what's Whitnal thinking? About the decision to run?"

"He agrees with the captain."

"Not everyone does," she said. "I hear rumblings some civilians think there should have been a vote."

"And you agree?" Asher chuckled. "How do they think that will pan out?"

"I don't agree, but Whitnal should deal with his people. The military will follow orders. The civilians need to toe the line."

"Don't say that kind of thing outside these walls," Asher said. "The moaners will get over it soon enough. Whitnal will make sure the message is crafted to help them understand the truth. Who grumbled?"

"Not on your life," Pen said. "If they'll get over it like you say, then I see no reason for you to get names."

"If I gave you a reason, would you tell?"

Was there a reason she'd believe? If she told him about Mellie and friends, what would he do? Would they be labeled for life as troublemakers? "I can't think of anything you can say that would change my mind."

"Fair enough." He stood and nodded at her terminal. "Keep looking at the feeds, but don't say no to our offer until you've spoken to the captain."

"Fine. Just leave me alone to think."

9

She didn't leave her quarters until the next morning. The flow of new information had slowed, and Pen couldn't draw any more conclusions. The scenario was still trying to account for the placement of the dead, and Pen figured it would run out of permutations soon. She couldn't see a hint that the damage was an accident.

The analysis had created a list of elements that didn't fit what they knew about the construction of Kalin's ship, so they may have asked him for input already. She didn't know enough about chemistry to figure out what was important.

She needed breakfast and she needed to stretch her stiff body. And she needed to report for duty soon. One thing that had changed since Asher's visit was her decision about Kalin and the girls. She needed to kick-start them into acceptance of reality. If she didn't act, they would try to convert the wrong person to their cause. And Kalin needed something more than the details of the attack to focus on so everyone would benefit.

She showered and changed to her uniform before leaving.

The corridors were almost empty today. Perhaps a good sign, or perhaps the civilians were plotting in secret. She laughed at the thought. It was ludicrous to think the news had changed everyone into rabble-rousers overnight.

Kalin sat alone in the dining hall. Pen grabbed a breakfast sandwich and coffee before joining him.

"Morning," he said when she sat beside him.

"How are you?" It sounded feeble, but Pen couldn't think of anything else.

"Tired. I worked with the data all night. You?"

"I watched all night. I guess we're going to have a lot of tired people around here today. Did you find anything?"

He nodded and looked down at his breakfast before looking up. His eyes were bloodshot and his skin ashy. For someone who stated so strongly he didn't care about the dead, he looked like he was grieving.

"Your analysts tried to prove it was an accident," he said. "They couldn't. There are some elements I can't verify, but they think they can use them to help track the attackers."

"I hope so," she said. "It will help people get over their feelings about the decision. Maybe help them feel safer."

"Pen, it is not that easy. What else do people have to think about?" He looked around the room before continuing. "If I took one of your scout ships, I would go looking for this evil thing myself."

"How?"

"That is what keeps me here, mostly," he said. "And I know inside I cannot do anything useful alone."

Okay. Pen let go of the sudden tension that came with his words. At least she didn't need to worry Kalin would do something stupid.

"If people had something else to think about, would it be better?"

"You have something to use as a distraction?" Kalin's eyes brightened. "Yes."

She wouldn't give him specifics, leaving the details to Mellie if she wanted to share; if she agreed. Pen wasn't sure how the girls felt about Kalin.

"I know some kids who are very unhappy," she said. "Life changed for them a lot in a short time. I wonder if you could help them gain a bit of perspective."

"You meant if I had a distraction?"

She tried not to blush, but her face heated anyway. "I guess I'm not so good at lying. Maybe I should tell Asher I don't have the basic skills and he will leave me alone."

"You must tell him directly what your decision is, when you make it."

How does he know I haven't?

"Yes, but these kids need some help and you need something more positive to do. Tell me I'm wrong."

Kalin wouldn't meet her eyes. If it meant he was thinking it over, she would wait.

"Why me?" Kalin finally asked. "A distraction is a good idea, but why would I be good for this one? I'm not experienced with children."

He was halfway there. "Teenagers, not little kids. I thought since your life has been totally upended, they might realize how little they've got to complain about. In fact, they should be happy we are not going after the attacker. When we land somewhere, they can reunite with their friends."

"I do not understand this expectation you people hold that the world will bend to your needs," he said.

"I don't think that."

"Okay, not all of you, but so many."

"I don't know how your people didn't argue more," she

said. "It's the way we work. But I worry for these girls. Rebelling now will follow them for life."

"Girls? That makes it less likely I will succeed." He laughed. "Okay, I will try. But not now. I must get some sleep. Your analysts will be calling me back soon and I need to have a clear head."

"Good," Pen said, relieved. "I'll check if they are willing to talk to you."

He laughed again. "You mean this may all have been for nothing? Life here is very confusing."

Pen started eating as soon as Kalin left.

The sleepless night was starting to catch up to her before she finished her meal, so she grabbed a second coffee to go and headed out. Her temporary assignment wasn't urgent, but she did need to catch up on procedures.

"I'm glad I caught you," Jo's voice cut through her concerns.

"On my way to report. Can it wait?"

"I'll be quick." He was upset about something. Jo could never hide his feelings from her. Others would not notice the tightness of his shoulders, or the way he checked around before he spoke. "I saw Asher coming out of your place last night."

"And you waited until now to ask me about it?" He'd been stewing all this time. Why? He would normally have been doing the same as her; trying to find information in the data. "Why didn't you join me?"

"I was on my way to do that," he said. "Then I saw Asher."

"Did you find something?" If he was coming to her, did he have any insight to share?

"No." He leaned against the bulkhead. "Did you tell Asher no to the job?"

"I've told him more than once and he won't listen." Why didn't he just leave it alone? She didn't have time to deal with his hurt feelings along with everything else going on.

"Did you tell the captain? He can make them stop bugging you."

"I've been busy," she said. "The captain has more important things to do than babysit me."

"That's not true. Why are you so sure the captain isn't going to help?"

She tossed her empty coffee cup into a recycle chute. "I don't know. Maybe it's just because I don't like my assignment. But anyway, you can't tell me he's got time to solve a problem for me, one I could deal with myself if you let me."

"I'm worried. You know how persuasive Asher can be. What happens if the captain finds out before you end it?"

"You mean how low can he demote me? For crying out loud Jo, he's got me talking to self-absorbed teenagers when the future of the fleet is in jeopardy."

"Are you sure you are going to stand firm and not take Asher's job offer? The way you talk makes me wonder if you'll go out of spite."

Now he didn't seem to care if anyone heard. The corridor was empty, thank goodness. She didn't want to turn up for duty after a fight, but she wasn't ready to let him win. "Do you really think I would be that childish? Or maybe you think working with kids is changing me, making me more stupid?"

"I didn't mean that," Jo said. He pulled away from the wall and looked around. "I'm worried. I guess about everything, and your future is the only thing I feel like I can actually help with."

"But it's my future," she said, trying to keep her temper. "You need to trust me, Jo. Things are changing, but not that much. And I'll tell the captain, I promise. But not yet. I need to do this myself. If I want to get a better assignment, I need to prove I'm capable."

"I think the mission showed you were," Jo said.

She checked the time. "I have to go," she said. They needed more time to hash it out, and she had to report for duty.

"Just promise you won't say yes without telling me first."

Why did he think she would say yes? She kept saying no, but no one listened. "Fine."

She stepped past him and marched toward her duty station.

10

S   he walked toward her desk, ready to log on, but her
duty officer interrupted.

"Report to the captain's quarters, Tromarin."

"Aye, sir." She turned and left.

If Jo had told the captain about her job offer, Pen was going to kill him. Being called before the captain so soon after their latest argument was suspicious.

As she walked, Pen rehearsed her answers; pretty much what she'd said to Jo, but with a heap more respect. The idea of telling the captain she wouldn't follow orders made her stomach twist.

The door to the captain's quarters was open. Pen knocked on the frame and stepped inside. The captain was talking to Whitnal.

Pen stood straighter. If she was about to get a dressing down, she needed to brace herself. If she was about to be handed over to Whitnal, she didn't know what to do. Following orders shouldn't be this complicated.

"I understand you feel your current assignment is not appropriate to your skills," the captain said.

"The job is challenging, sir, but I'm sure you had a reason to think my skills were appropriate." Who told him?

"Good to know. Mr. Whitnal has an opportunity I think will fit your skills better."

Her training kept Pen from blurting out the facts of Whitnal's offer. She stared ahead like a good soldier.

"I assume you are aware people are upset at what they see as a bad decision." Whitnal gestured for her to sit. She ignored the offer. "Asher reported your comments to me, and you are right. The civilians are my responsibility, but if it were that simple, we would resolve the issues quickly."

They waited for her to respond. "Why isn't it that simple?" How do I say no?

"Not just the civilians," the captain said, "and not only one issue. We are rapidly losing the window to unite the fleet."

How would her becoming a spy help? Pen waited, afraid to say anything because she couldn't tell what the right thing was in all the options.

"You've worked with Kalin. To help him integrate," Whitnal said. "It shows a sensitivity we need."

"Kalin is still hurting," she said. If they thought she was successful, they were basing the assignment on a mistake. "He was making some progress, but I'm worried the discovery set him back. And I didn't do that much to help."

"Did he not agree to meet with some teenagers?" The captain picked up his pad and checked a note. "That sounds like progress."

"May I speak freely, sir?"

The captain nodded.

"How did you get this information? I don't want Kalin to think I broke confidence."

"Kalin told us," Whitnal said. "We've been meeting with

him since he came aboard. We all want him to find a home here. He told us about your efforts."

Thankful no one had been spying on her, Pen still felt a touch of betrayal. Kalin should have warned her. But that was for another time. She kept her eyes on the captain. "You said you have an assignment for me, sir."

He smiled at her coldness toward the civilian leader. "It will mean you report to both of us; can you manage that?"

"If required, sir."

"Good enough for you, Roger?"

"I trust in your training," Whitnal said. "We will make it something she can live with."

Pen wondered if he really was that patronizing or if she was simply being too sensitive.

"The assignment is to be the public face of unity," the captain said. "I guess it's a bit more than public relations, but essentially that is what it amounts to."

"Shouldn't it be a civilian?" Pen asked without thinking. "I mean, unity needs both sides of the divide represented."

"It may come to that," the captain said. "For now, you will be enough. The messaging will be clearly from both of us. We start with this ship; we are the most stratified, but eventually the entire fleet will be involved."

It was too big. Kalin was one-on-one and that barely worked. "Can I ask for help, sir?"

"Some things will be confidential, but we can trust your discretion with most messaging. You may include Lieutenant Bryman or any expert."

"Thank you, sir."

"Any other questions?" Whitnal asked. "You will have contact with us but your assignment starts when you leave this room."

Pen considered what she'd heard. When she left, what

would she actually be doing? And what did confidential mean? She asked both questions.

"You will be assigned to the communications team. They can access tools and other items you might need." The captain handed her an identity pass. "This will give you the authority you need."

"As for the more covert aspects," Whitnal said, "some of what you do is gather information. You should keep that detail to yourself. Communications must not leak. Even if you trust someone, don't share anything. If you need someone, you can talk with the... resources we'll make available."

So, Asher.

He'd slipped the spying stuff in. Pen looked to the captain to check if he showed any reaction. He was either too professional for that, or he agreed.

She gave up trying to avoid working with Whitnal. "My first task?"

"Report to the communications team and get settled in," the captain said. "Dismissed."

Pen saluted and left. Well, it was probably a step up from talking to teenagers. But why did she feel like everyone except her got their way?

THE COMMUNICATIONS UNIT was located next to the boundary of what used to be the civilian sector. The living and working sections of the ship were tightly clustered still. Ship management teams were working to reactivate some of the old living quarters to accommodate the survivors, and maybe the rules around reproduction would ease up in preparation for populating a new planet. But it would take decades to fill the abandoned section between living quarters and the core.

Pen sighed as she'd spent the entire twenty-minute walk thinking about issues and how she could possibly craft communications for all of them. She didn't have what it took to rebel against orders, so she had to try. And maybe rebellion was reserved for teenagers. At least Jo would be happy she wasn't leaving the military.

"Tromarin?" A female officer Pen didn't know looked up from her screen as she walked in. "Grab a desk and I'll be just a minute."

Pen couldn't see the woman's ID tag, but her insignia of special officer meant she must be the duty commander of the unit.

There were a couple of empty desks that didn't contain pictures or jackets or any other personal gear. Pen took the one nearest the door.

"Good choice," the woman said. She held out her hand to shake. "Janice Choi-Walker. Call me Janice. We don't stand too much on ceremony here. I pass on orders and take any flak."

"Pen. I've never been part of a specialist unit before."

"Not to worry, we'll cut you all the slack you need. From what I understand, you'll be working independently anyway. Let me introduce you to the rest of the team and then I'll show you the systems."

The rest of the team turned out to be four junior lieutenants named Dave, Sunshine, Chen, and Karl. They said hi and turned back to their work. The actual communications were sent and received in the next room. Janice told her she would meet them tomorrow.

"Don't worry about them," Janice said. "If you need help, they are there for you. If they need your assistance, I'm sure you'll do what you can without violating orders?"

Pen thought it odd that Janice made that point. Did

people here violate orders on a regular basis? "Whatever I can."

"Sorry, I could have put that better. We don't get new people very often. I guess I mean we're a curious bunch. Need to be in this job. Don't feel bad about telling anyone, including me, you can't share."

"Okay." If only her friends were as easy to put off. "So, how do I find information in the system? And how do I send communications out?"

Janice gave her the log in codes for the communications systems. "Start with the section on manuals. I'm betting you find all your answers there."

A day of reading manuals? Pen could see the screens around her all running the feeds. Most of the scouts were back, but a few still patrolled the wreck and sent back results for analysis. A few more headed to the edge of sensor range to keep watch for danger. "Shouldn't I be working on something to explain what all this is?"

"No point until you have the hang of things." Janice pointed out the coffee station. "Not great, but the dining hall is a long walk."

Pen poured a mug of coffee and sat at her terminal.

An hour later, she looked up to see most of the others were gone. It was quiet, and far from being bored, she was fascinated by the information in the manuals. There were directions on delivering information in more ways than she imagined. Less on how to gather it, but she guessed that was her snooping and spying duties.

The most important thing she'd learned from the manual was she didn't have enough information. That a communication which didn't answer some of the questions was worse than no communication. She figured the top three things people needed to know were; are we sure we're safe; where are we going; and how do we know we can live there?

The captain might have the answers, but Pen didn't get this assignment to parrot the leader's words. Janice and Karl were still here. What exactly did the comm team know?

11

After heading to the dining hall to bring snacks and coffee for three, Pen asked for a few minutes of their time.

"You don't need to bribe us," Karl said. "You can continue as long as you like, just not mandatory."

Pen grinned at him. Karl was about fifteen years older than her. If it wasn't for the sparkle in his eyes, she'd think he was a cynical old man.

Janice took a sandwich from the plate and bit in, nodding to Pen to start.

"I am lost," Pen said. "I didn't expect to hit the ground running. I guess I didn't get time to expect anything. But I have no idea where to start and I thought I would by now." *How did that spill out? She must think I'm stupid.*

"What did the manual say?" Janice asked. "It's been a while since any of us had to look in there, but I remember it being helpful."

"Yes," Pen assured her. "Unfortunately, whoever wrote it assumed some kind of education to start with. I can look up the terminology but... What do you know about what we're about to do?"

"You mean run away and find a nice hole to hide in?" Karl leaned back in his seat. His voice held no passion, so she hoped he was just being provocative.

"I mean actual facts. I have a fair handle on what people are talking about, and that's one of the takes on it. But I think we need to get out there pretty fast with more than a vague plan."

"Yep," Janice said. "People are going to start making shit up if we don't give them something. What did the captain say?"

"No details. To be honest, I don't want to go running to him right away unless I have to. Part of the job is to dig out information, right?"

"So, you want to present something to the captain for him to approve? Not just a bunch of questions?" Karl asked.

"Am I wrong?" Pen hoped not.

"No. What do you think the details need to cover?" Janice asked.

Pen recognized a test when it was right in front of her. Janice must feel a bit of resentment that Pen had been shoved on her team. At least she wasn't outright hostile. "From the muttering I heard about the announcement, most people want to know if a planet is ready for us. How will we be safe while we travel and when we land? And I guess, how can we be sure the enemy ship isn't just waiting for us to come together so humanity can be efficiently destroyed?"

"There will be a lot more questions than that," Karl said, "but it's a good start."

"So, where do we find the answers? I can't believe the captain has time to tell me, or even knows all the details."

"We have some of the official word," Janice said. "I'll

show you how to search the database. The info comes from officials, and a few people who pass us more of a non-official level of detail."

"You don't ever tell anyone that," Karl said. "We need those facts, and the higher ups need to believe they are in touch with the ship."

Secrets and informants? How long has this been the way things worked?

"Don't look so shocked," Janice said. "Our job is to communicate, and the official word isn't a communication anyone can swallow all the time."

"So, my answers will be in the database?" Pen didn't believe it would be that easy. "Official and rumor?"

"All I can say is that we don't have a planet in mind, but we've identified an area where one is likely. One that doesn't need a lot of preparation for us." Janice crumpled her napkin and stuffed it into her empty cup. "Thanks for lunch."

"So, where do I find the other answers?" Pen asked. She couldn't let the subject go. There was no time to mull over ideas. People needed answers now.

"First, look in the database, and then look through the transcripts of recent communications," Karl said. "I promise you'll find a lead."

"We receive all the transcripts?" Pen was glad she didn't need to send messages on the comm system if it was that open.

"No and yes," Janice said. "We can access them. You request through the process, or you make friends next door. So, the information is available, but not without asking. And you'll find most of it is in hard to decipher code."

Pen groaned. "How do we manage to send out timely messages?"

Janice led her back to Pen's desk. "It works. I have no idea how, but it does. You'll need to talk to the captain eventually, but I promise you'll find something in here to take to him."

As MUCH AS she tried to put in another all-night session, Pen couldn't keep her mind alert after another meal at her desk. She took printouts with her to her quarters but fell asleep before she scanned the first page.

12

The morning didn't bring any sudden insights. Pen wondered when the captain or Whitnal would demand some kind of output from her. She grabbed breakfast early and headed into work, feeling a bit guilty she hadn't talked to Jo, or Kalin, or Loke since receiving her new assignment. She vowed to change that as soon as she felt like she'd made some progress.

Her first action was to introduce herself to the people actually monitoring and facilitating in-ship and ship-to-ship traffic. The transmission security team worked right next to her unit. Their door was closed but her badge gave her access. Another thing she needed to explore: how much access did it give her?

Inside, two men sat in front of screens. They wore headphones and leaned over monitors that scrolled lines of data. They didn't turn away from their screen until she coughed to get their attention. "Sorry to disturb you," she said. "I'm new and I need some data."

"How did you get in?" one of the men asked. The other

turned back to his screen as if he didn't need to acknowledge anyone.

Pen waved her badge at the one who spoke.

"Shit. This is supposed to be a secure unit. What do you want?" He glanced at his screen.

"How do I access the raw data?" If he didn't need the niceties, then Pen would go along. "I need to do research and I don't want to interfere with your work."

"Appreciated," he said. "Just a second." He moved to another terminal and typed a few lines. "You have access."

"Why didn't you need my name and ID number?" She was grateful, but it didn't feel completely secure.

"On your badge," he said, pointing. "The rest I pulled from your file."

"How did you access my file?" *And how many other people can poke around in there?*

"We get access because it makes the communications efficient. Anything else?" He looked at his screen again.

"How do I sign in?"

"It's on your terminal now, no need for any other passwords. Don't try accessing on your pad; I didn't give you mobile access." He left her standing and went back to work.

Pen returned to her desk and saw a new icon on her screen. She set a timer to remind her to leave for lunch and dug in.

The number of communications between ships surprised her. Until a few days ago, only official comms went through. Then an explosion of personal and administrative messages. Now, as the fleet came together, there was more reason to talk and more people doing it.

She didn't want to poke around in people's private business, so Pen left the contents of those messages private for now.

The official and admin contents were interesting enough. The positioning data attached showed only two other ships moving. So they weren't running from the scene yet. She calculated the time it would take for the final two ships to arrive. Shit, they were sitting ducks for another couple of days. And that was only if they set out as soon as those ships arrived.

She added, *when do we leave*, to the list of questions to put to the captain. And then underlined the first question she'd written; *where are we going?*

"How long have you been here?" Janice asked.

Pen looked at the time. "About an hour. I got access to the communications raw data."

"You met Gary and Chris?" Janice chuckled.

"They seem very committed."

"Don't be fooled by their dedication. They don't need to stare at the screens all the time," Janice said. "They made a bet on who will find the most interesting communication. You can interrupt them if you need to."

Pen laughed. "I don't want to get in the way of a bet. I've found some interesting items. Do you have a minute?"

"Sure." Janice pulled up a chair.

"I thought the other two ships were much closer, am I missing something?" She showed her calculations.

"Looks about right. The message was vague intentionally. We don't want people counting the minutes."

"Any idea which direction we'll head?"

"You'll need to ask the captain. Let me see what you have for him." Janice ran down the list of questions on Pen's pad. "Pick out one or two that are critical. When you meet with him, he won't give you hours for an interview."

"But how can I do my job with so many gaps in my knowledge?"

"People aren't ready for a long, detailed lecture on our future," Janice said. "Short, rapid messages are best."

Pen remembered seeing something in the manual about that. "I guess I'll set up a meeting."

"You are doing fine," Janice said. "It hasn't even been a full day. Give yourself a break."

Pen wasn't sure the captain or Whitnal would agree.

WHEN SHE'D REACHED out to Wes Royce, the captain's aide, he'd told her the captain would come to her sometime in the afternoon. Pen really didn't want to meet him in the unit, because there were no private offices. It would have to do.

With no specific time, and feeling trapped by all the data, she decided to risk missing the captain and wander over to the dining hall, hoping she'd learn something by listening to people.

It was full. Pen checked the time; it was morning break for the day shift. She looked around. Kalin sat nursing a coffee in the corner, looking like he'd been there longer than a few minutes' break. If she had a chance, Pen would ask the captain to give him a job to keep him from brooding.

"Where have you been hiding?" It was Mellie again.

Pen resisted the urge to either snap her head off, or simply ignore her. If she thought one of those would work to keep the girl away, she would happily apply it. "Good morning. Is there something I can do for you?"

"Tell me what you are doing to solve our problems." Mellie turned to indicate her three shadows. "Nothing has changed since you went into hiding."

Something was pushing this girl to behave like she had authority. It wasn't the usual teenage assumption that adults didn't know the simplest things. Another thing for Pen to work out. "I'm sorry you thought I agreed to do something for you. I have a job and it doesn't include doing your bidding."

"Well, if you won't then we will. You'll regret making us go over your head. My mother is very important on this ship and she will make your life miserable."

Perhaps her mother and father were the problem; giving her an inflated sense of her standing. Pen no longer cared. Mellie wasn't looking for help; she was craving attention. Her friends were doing nothing to accept their situation. Most of the adults were trying to figure out how to keep them safe and alive and they still expected to be the most important thing in their families.

"I think you missed your lessons on how this ship works." Pen stood rigid as she spoke, looking directly into Mellie's eyes. "The military does not answer to the civilian authorities. We work together. If you feel the need to keep pushing for your friends to be returned to their home ship, I suggest you talk to your parents about it. If they are powerful, I'm sure they will find a solution that doesn't endanger our survival."

"Then why did you come to our class?" Mellie trembled with anger. Her cheeks flushed under the makeup.

"It was an assignment. The captain wanted to give you the whole story. Other officers went to other classes to do the same thing." Pen searched for a way to soften the humiliation. Mellie had failed in front of her peers, people she pretended to lead. "You and your friends seem intelligent, so I'm sure you'll figure out how to move on."

It didn't stop the trembling. Mellie leaned in and glared at Pen. "We will."

Pen let her have the victory. "I'm happy to hear that."

Not willing to let the battle continue, Pen turned away to

get her coffee. She heard the girls muttering behind her. No one else paid them any attention and maybe that was one of the reasons they felt so powerless.

She sat beside Kalin without asking for an invitation. "Did you get a chance to talk to those girls?" She wondered if that was what depressed him. Although, he had many more reasons to feel hopeless.

"I've been busy," he said.

"Me too," she said. "I have a new assignment, how about you?"

That made him look up from his coffee. "You took the offer? What does Jo think about it?"

She rolled her eyes. "Not exactly that opportunity, but it seems like Asher got his way in the end. The captain assigned me to communications. And I report to him and Whitnal."

Kalin smiled at her, an expression with no joy. "So, everyone should be happy."

"Not what I would call it. So far, I've just been eyebrows deep in data. I have no idea what the captain expects me to produce."

"At least you are still in the military," he said, staring back at his mug. "You know things will change eventually."

"I guess. What about you? Did you get an assignment?"

"Other than hanging out with teenagers?"

"That was just an idea. And I think it's a bad idea now anyway. They don't need anything that makes them feel important; they need to settle down."

"So, I don't even have that," he said.

"What's been keeping you busy, then?" Pen wouldn't let him ignore her. She didn't care that he'd been one of the enemy; he was her friend now, and he was hurting. She wouldn't walk away and let him sink deeper into depression.

"The data. I got assigned to help with that. It's done now. I've told them all I can."

"The captain will give you something more if you ask." If he had a job, he'd have a purpose and a reason to be more optimistic.

"They didn't want to believe what I told them."

"Who? The captain?"

"No, the analysts. They didn't trust me. They double and triple checked everything."

"Of course they did," Pen said. He was reading things into normal actions. "They would have done that if Jo or me gave them answers. It's too important not to check."

"I could tell it was me they didn't trust. They see me as the enemy and that won't change."

Could she shock him out of it? "So, you've been sitting here sulking?"

He looked at her again. "You think I don't have a reason for feeling like an outsider? A week ago you thought I wasn't even human."

"That's not true," Pen said. Then, realizing he didn't believe her, she added, "okay, that is true, but not you personally. We didn't think any of you were human. We had no reason to think it. What did you think we were?"

"We always knew you were human," he said. "Just not the same as us. You were the adversary. We were fighting evil, godless people."

"Is that better than thinking you were aliens? Are we godless, evil people?"

Kalin sighed. "No. Godless yes, but I don't see evil. You didn't leave me to die."

At least if he isn't stuck in his old belief, there's hope. "Have you seen a counselor?" He shook his head. "Okay, come with me. No. Don't argue. What you do in the session is up to you, but you are going to one."

"Don't I need an appointment?"

"Don't sound so hopeful that you can wiggle out of it." Pen checked her pad. "I just made one."

She led him from the dining hall toward the medical section. "Promise me you'll try?" she asked as they stood outside the counselor's office.

"Why do you care?" He wasn't looking at her but staring at the door as if it was a trap.

"I look after my friends," Pen said. "Promise?"

He nodded and Pen decided that was the best she would get. She watched him as he walked through the door before returning to her station.

13

On her way to her desk, Pen passed Gary as he left. What happened to his game with Chris?

Janice was on the phone. The four other members of the team were sliding into their seats.

"Did I miss a meeting?" She sat at her desk.

"Just a quick update," Karl said. "Nothing to worry about."

Pen wondered how he knew what she needed to worry about. At this point anything could make a difference. "You never know. It was important enough to pull Gary away from his screen."

"Check with Janice." Karl turned away, focusing on his own screen. Pen saw a partial memo displayed but didn't push for details.

She thought they were friendly earlier, but maybe something had changed, or she didn't know how to read people. Janice was still talking to someone, so Pen turned back to the raw data, keeping one eye on her. Whatever it was, she'd find out. But first, she needed a way to sort through the stuff she had. The information was live, so maybe the update was on her screen waiting for Pen to find it.

Ten minutes later Janice finished her call. Pen was still trying to collate the information from the time she left the office to the time she returned. There didn't seem to be anything in timing codes or the location tags. She would be stuck reading the contents. That seemed like a dead end, but she remained determined. The captain should have assigned this to someone trained in data analysis, but he picked her, so she had to get it right.

"Janice," she said as she got up from her desk, "do you have an update?"

"Nothing for you," Janice said.

"Gary left his screen for nothing?" The words were out before Pen could stop them.

"No. I'm the judge of the contest," she said. "He thought he had something, but I didn't agree."

Then why does everyone else know? "It can't hurt to tell me." The captain would want her to hear everything without filter by anyone.

"It can, actually," Janice said. "You're drowning in data, right? You have a pretty vague idea of what might be important, yes?"

"Yeah, that's the biggest problem right now," Pen admitted. "But if I don't get all the information, how do I know what's relevant?"

"More information is going to make the whole thing worse." Janice must have seen the frustration on Pen's face. "You need at least one of two things. Either you need a specific mandate, or you need to figure out what kind of information is relevant. Until you do, let me screen it for you."

Only her training kept Pen from letting out her frustration. When she got up this morning, she was hopeful that she would find something; that she would be writing a message for the captain to deliver, and maybe a version for Whitnal. Instead, she was drowning in a deeper sea of unmanageable data, she'd been subjected to an attempted bullying, and she was worried about a friend. Being left out made everything worse.

"It's only day two," she said to Janice. "With respect, until I find a direction, I think I should see everything. I'll get a handle soon."

"I disagree," Janice said. She didn't pull rank out loud, but her tone carried weight. "I've been doing this for a very long time, Pen. I do know what I'm talking about."

The captain assigned me to this, not you. Keeping her thoughts inside, Pen said in her most rational voice, "I should clarify with the captain, he'll be here this afternoon."

"That's who I was speaking to, Pen. The captain told me not to pass on what Gary found. I'm sure he'll tell you the same thing." Janice went back to her work.

So, important enough to call the captain, but not enough to tell me about.

Pen couldn't think of anything to do about Janice stonewalling her. Pushing again might earn her a mark on her file and she had enough of those.

One thing she could do was stop relying on Janice or any of the others. Cutting herself off from their 'help' might give her a new view on what she had. Looking through all the information as it came wasn't going to get her anywhere. She needed to separate out the different kinds of communications. The captain didn't want help with official information. He needed her to figure out what civilians were talking about. Civilians and off duty military.

Pen opened and reviewed messages for ten minutes

before she realized she wouldn't be successful in any defini-
tion of reasonable time. She needed a program to search for
some kind of key phrases and narrow down the numbers.

It was basic coding; she just needed to think through the
parameters. Counting on people using words like *rebellion,
mutiny, or changing leaders* was naive. Pen parsed off an
hour's worth of messages for a test. In five runs of adding
and removing phrases to refine the results to something that
looked reasonable, Pen finally felt like she understood
the job a little. The last thing she wanted to do was to ask for
help again.

If she didn't have to wait around for the captain to drop
by, Pen would be out searching for the people who sent the
messages her search flagged. Even observing them would
tell her if they had bad intentions. She was no spy, but she
did know people. She would achieve the best results by
aiming at actual issues, not just grousing. And she wouldn't
ignore a real problem if she saw one.

There were five names on her list.

"Lieutenant Tromarin."

The captain's voice pulled her from designing another
search through the communications, this one tracking the
five people.

She stood at attention. "Sir."

"At ease," the captain said. "How's the new assignment
going?"

"Slow, sir."

"Any questions?"

"Yes, sir, but should we go somewhere more private?"

"Ask your questions and I'll decide." He didn't even look
around to check who was listening.

"First, when are you expecting me to produce the first
announcement?"

"In the next couple of days; too soon and we won't be addressing the real concerns. People need to digest what they heard. If you have something urgent before that, tell my aide."

"I can do that if you ask him not to push me off," Pen said. "I get it's his job, but I need access."

"Consider it done."

"I guess he will coordinate what I send with Whitnal?"

"I'll instruct him. That reminds me. You do this job for both of us, but I am your primary contact. Understand?"

That's a relief. "Understood."

"Is that all?"

Before answering, Pen checked to see what the others were doing. No one paid attention to them or they were doing a good job of hiding their eavesdropping. "Three specific questions, sir: When do we leave, how do we know we'll be safe, and where are we going?"

"Two days. *Tomorrow's Promise* has confirmed their ETA and we will give them a few hours to reorient. We'll be transferring a few more families."

Another problem, but one easily fixed. "Before they leave their homes, maybe you or Whitnal can explain why. It doesn't need to be in person, but some of the people we've already moved aren't happy."

"Which ones? We may be able to accommodate them before we start out. Once we're on our way, it will be a few weeks before anyone can find time to deal with problems like that."

Pen was sure the captain wasn't looking to punish people. He was concerned. But others might not take it that way, so she couldn't give names. "Not the specialists, but remember they have families, and you are pulling kids from their friends."

"Noted. As to the other questions, we can't say that we will be safe completely, but the techs developed a scan that will show the elements we found at the destruction site, and we sent scouts to patrol the largest area they can. And we are headed toward a system that looks promising. I will not give any more details than that. It puts us at risk."

Pen didn't dig into what kind of risk. She would find a way to craft the message so people felt they had all the answers. "I'll get to work, sir."

"So, you've accepted your role?" The captain smiled down at her.

Like there was a choice? "I fulfill all my assignments, sir."

"You'll need to show more enthusiasm than that when you face the audience, lieutenant."

"What?" She was delivering the message? "I thought you or Whitnal would present the messages."

The captain's grin increased. He was enjoying her discomfort. "I know. But I have this team to write my scripts. We need you to be the face of the ship, so to speak. Whitnal and I will be too busy running our transition."

Great! That was a whole new problem. "Yes, sir. But the first one should come from you."

"And you'll include an introduction of your role in that. We'll approve the content of future messages, but you will deliver most of them."

He didn't leave room for her to argue her way out of it. Now she missed her role as school visitor. "Yes, sir."

"Any other questions?"

"No, sir." None that sounded appropriate in her head, anyway.

"I look forward to seeing a first draft." He turned and walked away.

Pen sank down to her chair and stared blankly at the screen.

BEFORE SHE LEFT THE UNIT, Pen checked with Gary that she'd be able to access the data from her home terminal. He grunted, typed a few lines of code and then confirmed her access. He refused to give her access on her pad, telling her it wasn't secure, and she might leave the pad unlocked somewhere. She was too smart to tempt fate by saying she'd never be that careless.

Pen wasn't ready to knock on doors and ask the people on her list about the communications. Until the captain introduced her new role, she figured it would be too hard to convince anyone to talk to her. She spent a little time in the dining hall to see if there was more grumbling; no one cooperated by complaining to friends within earshot. The captain probably had it right; people were digesting what they knew. She couldn't believe deeper problems didn't exist. Surely no one needed a 'face of the ship' if only one communication would resolve the bitching.

None of her friends hung out in the dining hall this time. Jo was probably learning something far more interesting, like how scouts set a perimeter. Loke had his own work to keep him busy. Kalin, well, she hoped he was getting help.

Unfortunately, lurking wasn't clarifying anything. After trying for an hour to eavesdrop on conversations, Pen took a tray back to her quarters. Time to draft a message with the little she knew. And crawling through the comm data would be much more interesting at her own terminal.

She ate her dinner while she scribbled ideas on her pad. If she focused on the three top questions, what would make her less anxious? She projected the results on her wall and sat on her bed crafting a full script, including a few words for her to deliver after the announcement.

When that was done, she projected a list of new search terms. Seeing things from this angle proved useful. Pen lost her feeling of being overwhelmed, now she had some progress to hold onto.

As she looked at the list, Pen wondered why she didn't feel any of the concerns she was tracking. Yes, she was conditioned to obey orders, but not blindly. Why was she so confident in the leadership in this completely new situation? Even Whitnal. She might not like him, but she did trust him, mostly.

Thinking of Whitnal gave her an idea. Asher knew how to gather intelligence. Maybe he would give her some tips. The civilian part of her mandate worried her most. She'd been so focused on passing the game and getting her commission, Pen had never really been a civilian.

She sat up. Her mind was wandering. The job still looked too big; she needed a goal for tonight. Her brain could focus on getting to that rather than dragging up ideas about solving problems she couldn't even describe.

She cleared her pad to a new page and wrote. *Finalize communication. Practice delivery. Plan tomorrow.*

That was enough for tonight. And she could send the communication to the captain and Whitnal before she turned in. Doing so might leave her a bit of time to socialize too.

She projected the draft of the communication and started tweaking. Her mind still floated to planning tomorrow, but it was easier to refocus with a task to complete.

Her door chimed before she was satisfied with the results of her editing. A break would be great; maybe Jo came to catch up.

She released the door and looked up: Mellie and company.

Pen sat up and cleared the projection. "How did you know to come here?" Military personnel quarters should be higher classified than these girls could access.

"Can we come in?" Mellie asked, coldly.

"There's not much room. Maybe we can arrange to meet another time in a public place?"

"We will only take a minute," Mellie said. "Not all of us. Me and Jarl, if you don't have enough room."

The girl looked calm enough for someone intruding on a stranger. Pen stared at her, trying to assess her real mood. If this was another snit, she would deny her access. Mellie looked away. Perhaps in contrition, not coldness.

"Fine, just two." Pen turned off her monitor. There was nothing else in sight that the girls shouldn't see.

Mellie turned and said something to Aila and Flor. Both pouted but stepped back. So, this wasn't only Jarl's issue. Maybe this time she'd learn something to help her do her job.

"About this morning," Mellie said.

When she didn't continue, Pen crossed her arms and waited.

"I guess we were out of order. I'm apologizing for all of us, but Jarl is in the hardest situation. Aila has no ship to go back to, Flor's boyfriend might come back soon anyway."

"I appreciate the apology," Pen said. She knew there was more to it. None of these girls would come here to say sorry. "Jarl, I understand it's hard, but people are being transferred for a lot of good reasons."

"Yes. My dad made that clear when I got home from school. I won't be bothering you anymore."

Pen nodded. She wanted them gone so engaging was counterproductive.

"The captain called him," Jarl said. "I guess you told him about us."

Pen wished he'd warned her. But if it got the girls off her back, all the better. "Is that it?"

"You don't need to be a bitch," Mellie said.

"You came to my home, a place that you shouldn't be able to find. I accept the apology, but I have work to do."

"Fine. Kalin came to talk to us. You don't need to worry, he's happy to listen to us. He understands."

Kalin was too fragile to help them. Pen started to tell them to leave him alone, but caught herself before the words came out. Kalin hadn't shown any interest.

"Really? When did he talk to you?"

"This morning. Right after we talked." Mellie glanced around Pen's quarters.

She couldn't call them liars. But she couldn't let them get away with it. "I was with him later than that and he told me he wasn't going to reach out." Then she realized they had no way to know that she'd asked him.

"Fine," Mellie said. "We didn't talk to him. And we won't. We don't need a babysitter. We don't need a killer on our side."

"Why did you say he talked to you, then?"

"To get you off our backs," Jarl said. "Leave us alone."

Too tired to fight, Pen said, "I do as I am ordered. If the captain tells me to talk to you, I will. Now, how did you find my address?"

Mellie paled.

"You need to tell me the truth," Pen said. "I can always check."

"Aila's dad has access to it," Jarl said.

"So, you used his passwords to obtain information on an officer?" Pen made her voice hard. This was a big violation and could put Aila's father in serious trouble.

"Yeah," Mellie said. "But you can't prove that, so don't bother threatening us."

Pen smiled. "We can prove it. Maybe not that you accessed the directory, but Aila's dad did. And you are here. If I want to make a big deal about this, he would be in trouble. The kind that gets you in the brig."

Jarl's eyes widened, all aggression gone. Mellie pretended she didn't care, but she couldn't meet Pen's eyes.

"I won't this time," Pen said. "But if you cross the line again, or if you hurt Kalin in any way, I will complain to the security team. Are we clear?"

"Yes," Jarl said. "Mellie, come on, we have to tell the others."

Pen watched until they turned the corner before closing her door. She would talk to Loke and let him deal with Aila's dad. With luck, he'd ground her forever.

14

The door was chiming again. Pen opened her eyes. She'd fallen asleep while waiting for the results of her last search through the data.

She wasn't going to be ambushed again; until last night, only people she knew came to her door. Now that her address was out, she wasn't going to be so lax. Pen checked the small camera outside her door. Jo.

"Come in," she called, turning off the displays and closing her terminal.

Jo stepped in and looked around. "What are you up to?"

"Can't tell you." She wasn't alert enough to keep track of what would be safe to tell him and what wouldn't.

"Have you had breakfast?"

"Not yet. I was going to get something and eat here."

"Join me and Loke," Jo said. "We miss you."

"No, you don't." Pen laughed. "You want gossip." She felt her stomach rumble. Dinner was a long time ago, and small.

"True. Your new detail is interesting. What time do you report in?"

If she stayed in her quarters, Pen would just be grinding

through the same useless information. The captain and Whitnal had her first announcement. They would find her with their changes and additions if they wanted her. "I don't need to check in."

"What?" Jo rolled his eyes. "How do you land a gig like that? If I'm thirty seconds late reporting for duty, I get a lecture."

Her stomach rumbled again. "I need a shower. I'll meet you in the dining hall in twenty?"

"See you there."

SHE MADE it in fifteen minutes. The thought of breakfast with people who didn't try to bully her or give her impossible assignments was what she needed.

Today, she'd stay away from the unit until later. She would find Asher and get some tips. She'd track down Kalin to make sure he was okay. She knew that sinking deeper into streams of data was not the way to do the job. If only she could figure out what would work.

She smoothed her uniform as she hurried along. Did she look right for the presentation? She groaned. Another thing to worry about. Now that she was the face of the ship, she had to think of her appearance.

Thankfully the girls were not in the hall. Pen didn't trust them to leave her alone and didn't trust herself to face them again without snapping. She needed a success before more conflict.

She placed her tray on the table and sat next to Jo. "What's going on in the big world? I've been so focused on getting oriented to my new job, I feel like I'm losing track of everything else."

"It's only been a day," Loke said. "People are still looking for answers. Isn't that your new job?"

"How did you find out?" Was she wrong about the assignment being kind of secret until the announcement?

"You forget, my people are like a ship within a ship. They send me out to meet with the other leaders."

"Were you part of the decision to assign me?" He could have warned her.

"Not the decision at all. I would have suggested you if they asked, but all they wanted from me was feedback on the idea. And I gave Whitnal my proxy; I've got enough to do without dipping into politics. So, you are the new mouthpiece?"

That made it sound sleazy. "You'll hear the official word today or tomorrow." Pen looked at Jo. He didn't seem surprised. "Did you tell anyone?"

"Just Jo. I know the news has to be controlled," Loke said. "How is it going?"

"I can't figure out why you think I would be good at this," she said. She trusted Loke and Jo, but she wouldn't tell them any more than she needed.

"People like you," Jo said. "You listen to them. I agree. They chose the right person."

"Not everyone likes me," Pen said. "Loke, do you know a girl named Aila?"

He nodded.

"If I tell you something, will you let me decide if it needs to become official?"

"Sure. She's flexing her muscles lately, but she's a good kid. And she is highly intelligent."

"She used her father's access codes to find me."

Jo straightened and Pen realized she'd just assumed he would let her deal with the problem. "Settle down, I handled it. I promised not to get her in trouble, but if you could make sure she doesn't find a chance to do anything like that again, or something worse."

"I'll talk to her dad. Thanks for not reporting her; like I said, she's a good kid. Since we arrived, she's listening to her new friends more than her own sense."

One thing accomplished. "I also need some help with learning people's real concerns."

"You want us to spy?" Jo asked. "Is something going on?"

That was the real question. Pen couldn't tell him any details because she didn't have any. "I don't know. I can't believe I was assigned this job just to deal with a bit of grumbling. The captain can answer people's questions without me. There must be something."

Loke glanced at Jo. "No one told me to keep this confidential, but I don't want to screw up." He rolled his shoulders. "If I don't get things right, I'm afraid the rest of my people will lose any meaningful work and become passengers because no one trusts me. So you can't tell anyone, or even let anyone guess you heard this."

Pen wondered if Loke worried about her, or if the words were aimed at Jo. "I'll be learning a lot of stuff I have to keep to myself," she said. "One more won't hurt."

"I won't do anything that puts the ship at risk," Jo said.

"Good enough." Loke looked around and beckoned them closer. "In the meeting, they said it was because so many changes were coming. That people wouldn't just accept decisions. A preemptive move. Giving people a way to release their fears would stop them getting out of hand."

"That makes sense," Jo said. "Why a secret?"

"I'm getting to that," Loke said. "I got the feeling there was more. The way Whitnal and the captain delivered the information seemed orchestrated. Whitnal came across as smooth, but I don't think the captain is practiced at it."

So, it isn't only me. "Any guess?"

"The captain wouldn't keep something important from us," Jo said before Loke could answer.

"Of course he would," Pen said. "It's his job."

"Yeah, to keep us safe," Jo said. "Not like Whitnal. He does everything for power."

Pen didn't like that the two men were working together either, but the captain could take care of himself. "Loke? Any idea what they want?"

"Nothing I would bet money on, and I don't think they will tell me. But I can guess."

A guess from him was better than the nothing she had. "Your ship was set up differently, right? No division between military and civilians?"

"See? I told you this was the perfect job. You make connections faster than anyone I know. I think you can't imagine what could be coming because you have so much trust in the military and distrust of the civilians that it makes you blind."

"It's not just us," Jo said. "If a civilian did the job, the military would be suspicious. So what does your different structure tell you?"

"I know that people can do stupid and dangerous things if they feel threatened. The captain is right to start forming alliances with Whitnal. We're facing a huge threat and not everyone will simply follow orders. And I'm not only talking about civilians."

"People might mutiny?" Pen felt the truth in her words. No one on *Dark Prospect* would have entertained the idea a week ago. Now they knew there was a real and powerful enemy out there. Now the fleet was coming together after generations of staying apart. Too many changes.

"Not just one mutiny," Loke said. "People will fragment into different interests. We dealt with it a lot on my ship. And each time we transfer people between ships, we make it more likely that someone will see an opportunity."

The relief that she wasn't imagining things was tempered with the realization that the problem was bigger than she feared. "I need to know what people are grumbling about," she said. "It's my job to head off any problems."

"I'm not spying on people," Jo said. "But I'll pass on anything I hear."

"I don't need names," Pen said. "We don't know what will happen and people need to just gripe."

BACK IN HER QUARTERS, Pen checked for messages from the captain. Nothing yet. The discussion didn't help her find clues in the results of all her searches. As much as she didn't want to make a public speech, she wanted to get it over with so she didn't need to worry any more.

She cleared the information on the communications into a folder and started again. What if there were no messages in the time period she searched? Running a query on live data would take longer, but it was probably a better use of her time.

She looked over her search queries and thought about what Loke said. If people were already planning mutiny, maybe she could come up with a few more words and phrases to add. She combined some of the terms. Looking for the term 'disagree' wouldn't be specific enough. 'Different, disagree, wrong' might narrow things down.

Pen set the query running and turned to another task.

She wasn't going to spend today waiting for a call from the captain or reading lines of message contents. Time was passing and she needed to act. She sent a message to the captain's aide asking for a meeting.

Her terminal pinged. If meant the query was done, it was too fast. Pen held out no hope that the results would be of use. She finished her notes, ran the encryption and then turned to the screen displaying data. Only a hundred results. Her pessimism faded. At least it wouldn't take long to read through.

As she read, Pen flagged anything that seemed promising. None of the messages read as outright plans for overturning the leadership, but a few looked suspicious. After an hour she had narrowed the results to fifteen messages flagged. Of those, four were between people on *Dark Prospect*; she made a note of the names involved. On a second read, six of them turned out to be between the same two people; a reread of the contents made Pen blush. They were conducting a hot and highly experimental affair. Those she deleted. Five messages left. The location information showed communication between the same locations on *Dark Prospect*, only one with no destination ID. Something sent out into space?

The remaining tracing details were sparse. Pen checked the personal signature and a shiver crossed her shoulders; it didn't exist. The authorization code also proved false. Finally, she'd found something. But what was she going to do with it? She opened the contents and her excitement crashed: encrypted. Then she smiled; people didn't encrypt innocent messages.

15

The first thing she needed was confirmation that it was something. Maybe there were messages like this all the time. That was why new assignments were harder; so much knowledge wasn't in the manuals. So, step one was to check with Gary or Chris.

Pen set the common decryption programs running and headed out for the communications unit. She walked past the entrance to her room and straight into Gary and Chris's domain.

Gary looked up and then elbowed Chris. "Your turn."

Chris grunted and swiveled his chair. "What?"

"Do all messages carry valid authorization and signatures?"

Chris leaned back, suddenly interested enough to consider her question. "I'm guessing you found some without? Yes, it happens."

"What do you do about them?" She looked around for another seat, but there weren't any.

"We take a look. They are always about gambling, or affairs, or other petty stuff. Hasn't changed much since the other ships joined us. I guess, only that now the messages go between ships."

"Are they readable? I mean, not code?"

"Some are but the codes usually break pretty easily." Chris glanced over his shoulder, then leaned forward and dropped his voice. "What did you find?"

He was hoping she'd help him win the bet with Gary. *Not a chance.* "I'm breaking the encryption right now. Do you report this stuff anywhere?"

"It's in a summary. No one cares. Or no one cared, I guess."

"Is there a way to flag these codes?" Pen asked. If there was, her job would go faster because she wouldn't need to wade through the whole flow of communications.

"We tried. It slowed the system too much. The program had to check the authorization code against a list. Too much traffic for the process to be worthwhile."

Pen glanced at the screen showing the flow of messages. They ran up the screen too fast for her to count. There had to be a way, but it wasn't going to be on the live stream. "Did you ever find one that you couldn't decrypt?"

"One or two," Chris said. "We sent them along. Never heard back. Don't really care."

"Where did they go?" That would be her next stop.

"Hang on," Chris said. He turned to a terminal to his right and typed something in. "The last one was three days ago. We sent it to security." He glanced at Gary again. "Will you keep information to yourself?"

"You mean help you win?" Pen wasn't going to be slowed down by agreeing, and frankly she didn't care who won the stupid bet.

"That would be nice, but I figure if it's juicy enough for that, it will be classified way beyond my access. No. I might be able to tell you something else, but this is not exactly on the up and up."

"Unless it's something that endangers the ship, I'll keep my mouth shut."

"Okay. The message was forwarded to the civilian security team. I put a tracker on it just in case... you know."

"Yeah. That actually might help." Pen knew who to get to on that team. "Thanks."

Chris turned back to the communications stream as if she didn't exist.

PEN REACHED out to Asher for a meeting; he didn't answer. She left a message and decided if he didn't return her call soon, she'd start hunting him down. The decryption was still running if the monitor she'd installed was working. The program would go through every known code until it found the key or got to the end. Because she wasn't part of the security team, her authorization didn't come with a computing priority, so the searches could take all day. She didn't plan on sitting in her quarters or at her desk, waiting.

If she thought it would work, Pen would happily ambush the captain and ask him for details. There was no way unauthorized, unsigned messages were traveling without him knowing. The fact that he hadn't already told her was worrying.

Who else might help?

Neither Loke nor Kalin would have the right access. Jo might if his duty rotation put him in security. But she wasn't going to hold their friendship hostage to make him talk to her. He knew what she was looking for, and he would tell her if he found something.

Great! Her plan to stay out in the public spaces wasn't

going anywhere. And neither was her assignment. Everything sat on hold until she heard from the captain about the announcement, or read the messages, or met with Asher.

Only one of those was in her power. Asher could be anywhere. That didn't mean she couldn't find him.

IT TURNED out to be easier than she expected. Asher was in the observation lounge and alone. Pen marched over and sat beside him without waiting for him to acknowledge her.

He finished whatever he was doing on his pad then looked at her. "Congratulations."

"How did you know?" She rolled her eyes. "Never mind. Whitnal. Does he tell you everything?"

"I don't think so, but then I can't tell. Don't worry, he told me because he wants you to use me." He turned to nod at the screens. "People think this is a live feed, right?"

"And you are about to tell me it isn't?" Why would someone worry enough about the screens to interfere?

"Almost. The feed goes through an algorithm looking for anomalies. Do you think that's wrong?"

"It's wrong to call it a live feed if it isn't." Now Pen worried about what they were filtering.

"It isn't officially called that. It's an assumption that took life and no one spent energy clarifying." He turned to her again. "Answer my actual question: Are we wrong to clean the data?"

When Pen looked at the stars and black currently displayed, her response was different from her first thoughts. She tried to find evidence of tampering. Whatever they took out must be something critical to use resources. "It depends. If we relied on what we could see, and people found out it wasn't true..."

"And is there a reason to justify the editing?" Asher kept pushing.

Why was this important and how would it help her? Asher was trying to make her learn something, but what? She trusted the captain to make decisions like this. Maybe Whitnal too, but not as reflexively. They both wanted the ship, the fleet now, to be safe. They just took different approaches.

"If showing the unaltered feeds would cause fear. If the normal view is not like this." She waved her arm to encompass the entire wall. "Calm and boring. People don't come here much because the view doesn't change."

"Good work," Asher said. "Space is full of shit flying around that doesn't affect us. The scouts suggested it when they first started publishing the data. If we removed the filter, you'd see asteroids, comets, space debris, all looking like they are flying at the ship. But it's the view from the scout, right? They dodge and we deal with what won't simply miss us."

"But people would forget that." Pen closed her eyes to try to imagine what Asher described. "They would believe it was coming at us." Now that she understood, Pen wondered how she could have believed the live description. But Kalin had been here. He believed.

"Now you understand, right?"

"Yes. Whatever I do, it's not going to be about the total truth. I mean, not all about the truth. People need to feel secure. And right now, they don't." She took out her pad and showed the message she'd written. "Did I get it right?"

He read the screen and handed her pad back. "Almost, but they'll make a few tweaks and you'll learn."

"I wish they'd get on with it," Pen said. "I am not looking forward to my first appearance."

Asher laughed. "You'll be fine. Although I am not expert at being in the public eye. The shadows are my environment. If Whitnal gives you advice, listen. The captain isn't used to people who don't just obey. Whitnal knows more about persuasion."

"Okay. Thanks."

"But that's not why you tracked me down. What do you need?"

"You are pretty relaxed for someone who lost your new recruit."

"I'm used to compromise. Maybe I haven't lost you. Maybe this is just a delay."

Pen shook her head. "I don't see it happening." She switched to another file on her pad. "This is why I came. I guess I can trust you to keep quiet until we learn more?"

Asher didn't look at the file. "You should have asked that first. It's best to know if people are lying to you before you take the risk. But, yes. My job is keeping secrets." He took the pad back and looked at her notes.

Pen watched his reaction as he read. She'd listed the key points. No names. Only the facts and her suspicions.

He handed back the pad. "Do you have a suspect?"

"Not enough to point to one that I can support. But would Whitnal do something like this?"

"If he thought the captain was putting the ship in danger, then yes, but he's trying to build a future. When we land, the civilians will hold the power. He wants that, and he needs a peaceful journey so he's in position to grab leadership the minute we are planetside."

"Then how do I find a good suspect?" All the frustration of the last two days came out with the words. "I don't know how to go any further."

"That's why you came to me." Asher checked the time. "I

need to go to a meeting soon, and I need time to think about what you showed me."

"So, I just sit around waiting for you, too?"

"You'll hear soon," Asher said. "I promise you'll look back on this with envy. If you've found what we think, you'll be eyebrows deep in action. And you need to practice your announcement. And you should polish your image a bit."

"What's wrong with how I look?" She was wearing her uniform.

"First, most of your audience isn't military. So being all spit and polish won't make them listen."

"I have to wear this," she said. "My other clothes are too casual. And I'm a lieutenant, not a civilian."

"Not saying you should hide that, but... Look, you could wear some makeup, and maybe get your hair looking, I don't know, slicker?" He picked up his pad and tapped a few keys. "I've sent you a contact. She can show you what I mean. It's hard to explain. You will look like the perfect officer when she's done and you'll show as more human than a cold military drone."

"I'm not human?" She laughed. He looked like he was going to speak, so she added. "I get it. The uniform makes a solidarity statement. You want me to look like an individual too. Am I right?"

He grinned. "See? You have the potential."

"So when can I expect to meet again?"

"Give me a few hours," he said. "In fact, let's set a time now. How about zero-one-thirty? It'll be quiet."

"Where?" There was no place on the ship she was aware of that they could guarantee was empty.

"How familiar are you with the abandoned areas?"

She'd been there a total of three times. Twice as a kid after a dare and once officially to locate a missing child who'd done the same. "About as much as the average person."

"I'll send you some schematics. We'll meet in the old theater. Don't let anyone know. Not Jo, not anyone."

"Like I said. If it doesn't endanger the ship, I'll keep your secret."

"And I need you to stop investigating until we meet. We can't get in each other's way."

Pen thought about her decryption program. That wasn't investigating, and she wouldn't have time to act on any results. "Agreed."

"Good enough. Now I have to go."

Alone in the observation room, Pen realized she had no interest in the display.

Her message pad pinged. The captain. She opened the message. *Announcement at fifteen hundred. From Whitnal's office. Amended contents attached.*

Her anxiety didn't drop because she had a time. It increased and made her lightheaded and a little sick. Her plans to stay away from the office were lost. She figured Janice or her team would be able to give her the best advice to prepare.

Her pad pinged again. Asher's image contact. *Come to my quarters now. I promise it will only take 30 min.* The address was attached.

If her pad wasn't going to ping with the decryption results, Pen figured she had time to do a little polishing.

AN HOUR later she stepped out of Zara's quarters, her face looking smooth and perfect, her hair shining and her stomach still full of butterflies. At least she'd be able to repeat the look. Zara made her practice until she was satisfied.

Now she was ready for her mental polishing. If Janice could do as much to her mind as Zara had done to her physical appearance, Pen would be ready.

Her pad pinged. Finally, the results of the program. *Code does not conform to known decryption processes.*

Disappointment added to her feelings of inadequacy. Pen wasn't used to this absence of expertise; it made her question her actual abilities. She sighed, trying to get rid of the doubts that diminished her confidence. All the makeup in the fleet wouldn't help if she didn't believe in herself.

"Wow. You look... professional?" Jo walked beside her.

Pen looked at him sideways. "Don't I usually?"

"Yeah, but this is a whole different level. Are we about to meet a new Pen?"

"Same old me. Someone suggested I needed to look different for this new role." She hated keeping secrets from Jo, but with him she had a chance to talk to someone who didn't expect her to become a super communicator overnight.

"Asher?" Jo asked, his voice tightened. "I thought he'd leave you alone now that you have a new assignment."

Why didn't Jo just leave it alone? "Stop being that way. You don't know him. He's helping me. The captain is okay with me working with Asher." As she said the words, Pen realized

Asher let her assume the permission, and she hadn't checked with the captain.

"I do know him. He wants you to join him. No matter what happens, or what you say, he will keep pushing to make you leave the military."

The only person trying to make her decisions was Jo. "No. He's helping." She heard the snap in her voice and regretted it. Jo was only worried. "Look, I don't want to take his job offer. I do need someone to give me tips on the one I have. And I can't share most of what's going on. Asher has the skills and he's been cleared."

"I don't like not being the person you turn to."

"Are you jealous?" She'd never thought of Jo in that way. "There's no need."

"No, it's not that."

Pen couldn't bring herself to believe him completely. "If not that, then you don't think I'm smart enough to take care of myself?"

"Of course I do." He shrugged his frustration. "I don't know, Pen. I have this feeling of dread. Maybe it's because we can't talk about it. So many things changed since we came back from that planet."

"Our friendship hasn't." She tried to view this situation through his eyes. Both of them had assignments that meant they couldn't hang out as much. She had been too busy to miss him, but what if he'd been trying to figure out his new and upside-down world? "I need to deal with this on my own, Jo. I'm sure things will stabilize, and we'll go back to seeing each other. Unless you are out with the scouts when I have nothing to do." She tried to make the words a tease, but Jo didn't smile or retaliate.

"It might be too late then," he said. "I'm not kidding about feeling like something bad is going to happen."

"I'm sorry, Jo. I hope it will never be too late, but I have to go. You'll understand later why, but right now..."

"I get it. Please, be careful. Not only of Asher. You aren't safe with the civilians."

"What?" Now he'd gone too far.

"I don't mean they'll hurt you. Try to remember, you know the military life, and you can be reasonably sure who you can trust and mostly who you can't. Civilians look at things a different way. Don't get too comfortable."

"Okay, but do me a favor?"

He nodded.

"Let me figure this out. You don't need to monitor me all the time."

"Agreed."

He turned and left her outside the door to her unit.

Pen stepped inside and looked around for the duty officer. Janice was talking to Sunshine and Chen. She took a breath and let go of her annoyance. It didn't help her anxiety, but that was what she came here to resolve.

She walked over to the small group and waited for them to finish.

"I see you've learned about image," Janice said, glancing over Pen's entire outfit. "Good choice."

"Janice, she looks great," Chen said. He glanced at Pen again. "You only have a few hours to keep it looking like that, just don't spill coffee on your uniform."

"Thanks, Chen," Pen said. "I wasn't worried about that until now."

"You're welcome." Chen made to return to his desk.

"Wait," Pen said. "I need some advice. Do you have a minute? All of you?" They sat and Janice pointed to the one open chair. "Make it quick."

What had made Janice start acting so coldly? Her words

were fine, but the tone made Pen feel like she was simply going through the motions.

Keeping Asher's request to stop investigating in mind, Pen told them she'd run into some anomalies in communications. "Have you run into anything like that before?"

"What kind of anomalies?" Sunshine asked. She'd been quiet until now. Pen hoped it was because she was considering the problem.

"I can't give you details, yet," Pen said. "I know that doesn't help. But what reason would someone have to undermine the system?"

"Undermine?"

"Probably too strong a word. Working around restrictions might be the right term."

No, the right term would be the actual case. Pen kept her face clear of her inner conflict. "I guess I can think of a list of bad reasons, but what would make a good reason?"

"It could be official stuff," Chen said. "Some things need to be more than just encrypted. Would these anomalies make the message untraceable?"

"So far," Pen admitted. His suggestion didn't feel like the answer. But she couldn't rely on feelings. "I can open the messages. But I can't break the code."

"There are codes that scramble messages if they are opened by the wrong person," Sunshine said. "Maybe that's why."

"Oh, so it's impossible to find out what the message contains?" Pen wouldn't stop digging, after she talked to Asher, but impossible was much harder than she expected.

"With your clearance level, yes," Janice said. "I don't think we can help you if you can't tell us the details."

Pen couldn't until she had an idea of who sent them.

The people with the best access to do that were right in front of her. "I'll check with the captain."

"That's the best idea." Janice sent the other two back to work.

"There was something else," Pen said. She checked the time; fifteen minutes until she had to report for the announcement. "Any tips on not puking up my guts during my first address?"

Janice burst out a laugh. "That I can help you with."

JANICE'S ADVICE HAD HELPED, a little. Mostly the *breathe deeply before you go on* and *remember you are talking to people, not the camera*. Pen felt like she'd done a good job, the captain congratulated her, Whitnal shook her hand. It was over.

"I have some questions," Pen said when it seemed like they were dismissing her. "There are some things I need to clarify."

"Not today, Pen," the captain said. It was a shock to hear him use her first name. "Go see how people took the news. I'll send you a time tomorrow to meet. Just be happy this went well."

"The first reports show good response anyway. Pen has never been on this side of the process. She deserves to hear why we think it's enough for now," Whitnal said.

Pen held her breath waiting to hear if the captain would agree. If he only wanted her to follow orders, this was the moment she'd get confirmation.

"Roger, it's not easy to stop expecting obedience."

"Erik, that's why you have me. I'm not asking you to share state secrets here."

She felt like she was intruding on something. She knew

the captain's name, Erik Odsmundsen, but no one used anything but his title.

"We placed people in the audience to give us the initial reaction. It's good. But you will get more real reactions as people think about what they heard."

"Good to know, sir. Thank you, Mr. Whitnal."

"Don't be afraid to push back, Pen," Whitnal said. "Just not right now. Go listen and you can tell us tomorrow what you think we should talk about next."

Sensing she wasn't going to learn anything more, Pen saluted and left.

She wondered how people could have questions. The answers were clear. They were leaving tomorrow or the next day at the latest. They were able to track the elements left behind at the destruction so the scouts could send out early discovery of the enemy. She found herself thankful now that the observation feed wasn't live. If the scouts found something, it wouldn't give them much notice. But, at least the ship wouldn't plunge into panic.

And the captain had shown a graphic of the system containing their new home planet. Just not the actual location.

Two places came to mind. The dining hall and the observation lounge. There would be people in both where she could check on the reaction. She needed food and a nap before she met with Asher.

In the observation room, there were only a few people. No one was grumbling, but no one was talking with her around. In the dining hall, she received some applause and a few people drifted over to speak to her personally.

"Can you get me an appointment with the captain?" one woman asked. Pen pointed her in the direction of Royce, the captain's aide.

"What's the real story?" a man asked. He laughed, but Pen saw a shadow of fear behind the humor.

"You heard it, I promise," Pen said. "We'll learn more as we start moving, but for now, you know everything we do."

"You don't know where the system is? How far? What the closest star is?"

"I'm sure the navigators have everything they need to get us there," Pen said. "The details will come out as soon as we can." She smiled at the man and said, "Don't forget you can send your questions to me. I appreciate all the help you can give me."

"You may regret that, but I'll give you a day or two before I fill the inbox." The man laughed heartily this time, leaving Pen with more confidence in her abilities.

Mellie stepped into the space he vacated. Pen tensed.

The girl looked around and apparently decided against making a dramatic statement. "Can anyone send questions?"

"Yes. Gathering questions is the reason we created the inbox," Pen said. "I hope you take advantage of the channel."

"Oh, we will," Mellie said. "Don't think you can get away with hiding things." She marched away.

Pen answered a few more questions, then excused herself. She took a tray back to her quarters, removed her makeup and got ready to sneak into the abandoned area.

17

E verything on the ship ran twenty-four hours, but night was quieter. A remnant from their planet-bound history, and a preparation for a future living with night and day cycles. It meant Pen was mostly alone as she walked through the corridors. She would be early to their meeting as planned. A chance to explore the area was hard to ignore now that she was an adult. And she wanted to show Asher she wasn't going to just obey him.

She passed the dining hall before she met anyone wandering the corridors. A few civilians nodded at her as they passed. Being more recognizable felt odd. No more walking around as an anonymous military officer. At least they didn't hold her up with questions.

She noticed Kalin ahead as she passed the medical section. Before she caught up, he turned and entered one of the counselor units. Another positive. He was getting help.

This day was turning out to be a big move forward. Pen was sure Asher had some news for her. And some advice.

If everyone was more like her, Pen thought, they'd accept the new people they met and see the new reality as a positive. No one was taking Kalin into a quiet corner and beating him, but she'd seen the suspicious looks and the way they moved slightly away as he approached. Not everyone, but enough.

She could understand; he represented everything they feared for too long to accept him so quickly. But did they think Kalin posed a danger? His ship gone, he had nowhere to go. If they spent a few minutes with him, they'd understand how alone he was.

A tiny voice inside asked her if she truly believed he wasn't a danger. If she didn't suspect, even a little, Kalin was leading them to a trap. That they only had his word the wreckage was the last of his ships. That the bodies weren't prisoners used to bait the trap. She told the voice to shut up.

She turned toward the entrance. The sign on the door warned people against entering. The door code was third level security, but every school kid knew how to access the area. No one in charge seemed to care, perhaps because kids were too scared after their first visit to ever go back. Her new job had already changed the way she thought. She swore to fight the urge to become suspicious of everything.

There was no one in the immediate area, so Pen entered the code and slipped through. Inside, the only light came from the emergency fittings at intersections. It was hard to stay optimistic in the gloom.

The passageway ended in a three-way intersection. Pen strode to the end and looked in both directions; at this point she'd run back to the door when she was a child. Last time, she'd been part of a team and felt safe. Someone else gave directions and she couldn't remember them now. The theater was to her right according to the schematics. She turned left. Knowing what lurked in both directions might come in handy if they spent a lot of time in this section.

No dust. The area might be abandoned, but maintenance robots still managed the space. Expending a little energy meant avoiding catastrophic consequences of equipment failure in the future. And if they needed to re-inhabit, there would be no surprises.

Pen froze at the sight of movement ahead.

A monitor robot crossed the passageway from one room to another. She sighed and gave a chuckle, then realized her hand clutched her weapon. "Okay, maybe you didn't leave the panic behind when you were a kid."

The passageway was lined with living quarters. Pen realized she'd been thinking of it as a whole new section of the ship. Looking for some transition between living and absent. All they had done to cut it off was build a bulkhead and lock a door. Of course it made sense. When these quarters were used, it would not be a separate area, but an increase in civilian quarters.

If she remembered the schematic correctly, ahead were only storage and maintenance rooms. The bulk of the section was in the other direction, where she was meeting Asher. She turned and headed to the theater.

"NICE OF YOU TO COME EARLY," Asher said as she slipped through the double doors.

"How long have you been waiting?" Pen asked, determined to beat him next time they met.

"An hour." He laughed. "Always do a thorough sweep of your meeting places, Pen. Even the public ones."

"I'm not that paranoid," she said. "Do I need to be?"

"Do you want to be good at this job?" Asher pinned her with his gaze. "This isn't a hobby for anyone."

"I'm not your spy," Pen said with a bit more snap than

she expected. "Of course, I want to be good at my job. At my job, Asher, not yours."

"You are doing a version of my job," he said. "And you came to me, remember?"

Pen sat in one of the chairs. Standing and facing him made her combative. "I did. I just don't like suspecting everyone. It will cost me my friends, right?"

"It doesn't have to. Do you think your friends are going to commit crimes you'll need to tell the authorities about?"

Pen was about to say, absolutely not, when she remembered the little voice. "Jo? no. Loke? Not a crime, but we won't always agree on how things should go. Disagreement isn't a crime, right?"

"No, the opposite. Without disagreement, things go horribly wrong because the people making the decisions lose perspective. What about Kalin? Did you think I didn't notice you left him out?"

She looked down, ashamed to share her thoughts. "He's not a threat."

"No, you really don't think he's safe, deep down."

"He is alone. He's hurting and too many people look at him with suspicion. He's getting help."

"Yes, all good reasons to feel bad for him. If you can't see the problems he could make, then you need a new assignment."

It didn't mean she couldn't be his friend, Pen thought. Maybe acknowledging that the fears were valid would make her a better one. "If I look at it from a distance, not knowing what he's gone through is real, then yes, he looks like a danger. Also, it's kind of weird he has the run of the ship."

"Better," Asher said.

She told him what her nasty suspicious side had prompted on the way to the theater.

"And how would you answer the questions if they came from a civilian, or a fellow officer?"

"Or anyone," Pen said. Asher hadn't considered the whole non-commissioned part of the military, or the fact civilians weren't all equal. Or had he? She watched him observe her thought process. "You are a good mentor. Okay. If anyone asks why I believe he's alone, that all his people are dead, I'll talk about being there. You saw him when he realized they'd abandoned him. No one can fake that."

"Don't rely on your estimate of people's ability to lie. But you are right. I believed him. Still do."

"And when he heard the news about his ship, I was there. The news devastated him. It's why I made him go to a counselor. There's no enemy ship lurking. At least, not the enemy we know."

"It could still be the same one. The only thing that's changed is we know they are human like us."

"It doesn't matter what enemy we're avoiding. The plan we have is still the best option."

"We need to talk about this more," Asher said. "But before I get into what I found, you need a bit of training."

"No. I need that information now," Pen said. She couldn't delay for days.

"Relax. Give me five minutes to share a tip or two."

As much as she wanted to barrel ahead, Pen knew she needed help. And Asher was the only one offering it. "Fine."

"This is a hard lesson to hear, and an even harder one to learn on your own," Asher said. "The person you are looking for is rarely a surprise when you find them. And, yes, it's often the person who is acting like a villain. You end up proving what people suspect. But just as often, someone you trust without even thinking about it turns out to be the bad guy."

"Jo and the captain. But they wouldn't."

"Step back a bit," Asher said. "In this case, I'd be shocked if you proved they are doing this. Jo is a straight, boring good guy. And the captain doesn't need subterfuge; he's in charge."

"Jo's not boring," Pen said. "He's the responsible one."

"Exactly. The captain chose you for this assignment because you are still willing to bend the rules."

She couldn't deny it. "Okay. I'll keep it in mind."

"This won't be your only assignment, Pen. Things are changing and change can bring chaos. We can't afford to lose control. At least until we land."

Pen rolled her eyes at the thought of trying to corral people when they had a whole planet to hide on. "You said two pieces of advice."

"Don't isolate your friends." He laughed at her expression. "Yeah. This life is full of contradictions. If you let yourself drift away from personal connections, you'll fail. You'll lose compassion."

"Does that mean you have friends?"

"As surprising as you find it, yes. And you are one of them. And Jo. I'm not sure about Loke or Kalin yet."

Asher smiled as he talked, but Pen heard a ring of seriousness in his tone. Given his advice that the people you trusted could be the bad guy, she didn't take much comfort in being considered a friend. And the mean little voice said, *Asher could be hiding his real intentions.*

"What did you find?" She wasn't going to let him hold back any longer.

"Nothing concrete. It's clearly something, but I need more time to crack codes, or more input."

"So, I'm no further ahead."

"I didn't say that." Asher took a drive from his pocket.

"Knowing these communications are not legitimate is the first step. We'll crack them, but at least we know there's something to crack."

"I thought maybe you had more decryption software," Pen said, disappointed. "How much more data do you need?"

"Pen, we rarely achieve something fast in this line of work, and it's rarer that fast is equal to good. Step one, get enough input."

"How? It took me too long to find what we have. And it's not like they use the same fake codes."

Asher sat back and looked at her. "Do you usually get discouraged this easily?"

"No." The answer came out before she thought. "Not usually. I'm finding this job is too hard to grab hold of."

"Pen, you have to commit. Every time I don't give you what you want, you back off. You can do this job. It's all gray area and very slow progress until you have everything you need to act."

"I agreed to do the job," Pen said.

"That's not enough."

"Fine. I'll be all sunshine and butterflies."

"You know that's not what you need. Suspicion is healthy; patience is critical."

Did she break the rules because she had no patience? "Does it get easy?"

"You learn to control it," he said. "It's not like I don't want to rush ahead. I've simply had the opportunity to learn."

"Okay, I'll cultivate my patience. Now, how exactly do we find more data?" She hoped it wasn't by sifting through more obscure messages.

He held out the drive. "You need to plug this into the system monitoring all comms."

"That gives you access to everything."

"I added a code to pull out only communications with specific attributes."

This was a test of her trust whether Asher meant it to be or not. How could she be sure he wouldn't take anything but what they needed?

When Asher raised an eyebrow and waited, Pen realized she needed to work on her poker face.

When she didn't answer he said, "It will be faster than you going through the data."

"How do I know it's not just a grab for all sorts of information?"

Did he lecture her on patience so she would jump at something fast? Was he manipulating her? Was Asher somehow involved?

"Good," he said. "You suspect me, right?"

"Should I simply trust you?"

"No, but you also need to ask why I need to make you do this." He waited for her to think it through.

"It lets you hide behind me if we get caught." She shook her head. Too easy. "It's not about blaming me. You know I'd tell the captain everything and take my punishment. Protecting Whitnal? Yeah. You give him some distance."

"How likely is it Whitnal is behind whatever this is?" Asher pushed.

"Not very. If he wants to take over, he just needs to work the civilians up for when we land."

"Good. So why do I need you to do this?"

"You don't." It bothered her to admit she wasn't important.

"Exactly. I could do this without you. I'm giving you this to help you. We need to be allies, and me undermining you isn't going to make that happen."

"You can read everything going on in my head," Pen said. "You? I can't read anything. How do I get that good?"

"You start to rationalize keeping your thoughts to yourself. It just happens. And it happens faster than you think."

"Okay," Pen said. "Any specific place? And how long does it need to be there?"

"Any port," Asher said.

"Who sees it?" Pen would not let herself be cut out of the loop.

"You and me."

Pen held out her hand. "Give it. I'll take care of it by breakfast."

Asher made Pen leave first. She strode along the passageway and through the door to the inhabited part of the ship. There was no one there, but more light seemed to create more feeling of people.

18

Despite the late hour, Pen was starving. She headed for the dining hall thinking about how she'd install the drive. She knew where it would be unobtrusive, but she needed a distraction for Gary and Chris, or whoever else was on shift.

Three people were sitting together: Jo, Kalin, and Loke. Time to mend some relationships. Asher's lessons struck home, maybe not in a way he expected. To do this job, Pen needed her friends. And these were her friends even with her doubts. She ordered a sandwich and drink before joining them.

"I thought I was the only one of us with insomnia," Pen said as she sat.

"New assignment," Jo said. "I need to report in an hour for scout training."

"Does that mean you are going out on patrol?" Pen needed Jo here to keep her sane in a world of suspicion.

"Not for a few days," he said, "but the training is intense. I won't be around much during the day."

"I have no idea what my hours will be," Pen said. "We might end up midnight dinner buddies."

"I don't know whether to hope so or not," he said. "But you need to be where people are talking, right? I'm guessing during the day is more likely."

Pen wondered if he wanted her to withdraw. She might not be the only one with secrets. Thinking back, she realized Jo was very good at hiding his thoughts. Every time he took the blame for their escapades, he managed to look completely at fault.

"Are you keeping him company?" she asked. Making Kalin the focus meant she wouldn't be pushing at Jo.

Kalin looked up at her, breaking his habit of looking down, not meeting anyone's eyes. Did he do that because he didn't want to see the suspicion, or because he didn't want anyone to guess his thoughts?

"I don't sleep much. My people considered it lazy; only the sick or young got more than four hours. It's going to take a while to undo my conditioning. At least that's what the counselor said."

"Is the therapy helping?" Pen asked. She was surprised he'd mentioned the counselor; it wasn't taboo, but Kalin was closed off. Why did he? To disarm them? To make himself seem harmless?

"Too soon to tell," he answered with a shrug. "I have no experience with counselling, so I plan to take her word for it. Why are you up this late?"

"I had a meeting." A half-truth. She wasn't ready to test her ability to outright lie. "And I must check in early. Back to grabbing a nap and a meal when I can, I guess."

"You did a good job," Loke said. "Remember that. I think tomorrow you'll start to hear the real reactions. Don't check that inbox before you go to sleep."

Because there's something he doesn't want me to see?

It was hard work second guessing every statement. Of the three people here, Loke was probably the most likely to have a different agenda.

"Too late. I glanced at it. Three hundred items so far," she said. "I didn't read the contents. I'm planning to ask for help screening the emails. If I'm stuck doing it alone, I won't get anything else done."

"What else is there?" Jo asked. "I thought it was your job to communicate."

"Someone has to prioritize the issues," she said. "Who knows what might need my attention most."

Jo cocked his head. She hadn't fooled him.

Loke came to her rescue. "When the captain and Whitnal asked me to weigh in, it wasn't about the best mouthpiece, Jo. And you know Pen is the last person I would recommend for that."

"Many things about your life baffle me," Kalin said. "This is the most alien. People should obey, not question."

"If that were the case," Loke said, "you would be dead. You think Pen or Jo had orders to save your life? Just obeying isn't good. Things come up and someone has to make a decision."

"I think the fact that my ship and my way of thinking are gone, is enough to prove your way is better," Kalin said without any emotion.

"We came close," Pen said. "You were able to destroy so much of our fleet. It was only by chance that people survived. If we weren't on the rescue, we'd have continued on. You would have destroyed more ships. We wouldn't know about this new threat." She finished her sandwich as a reason not to keep talking. She needed to practice listening, not convincing.

"No point in talking about what might be," Loke said. "We deal with what is and keep moving forward."

Jo checked the time. "Gotta go. Wish me luck?"

"You don't need it," Pen said.

He grinned. "True, but it's always good to appear humble. You'll learn that, madam media star."

He walked away while she gasped for breath as a laughing fit overtook her.

PEN WASN'T ready to sleep. If she could install the device before going to bed, all the better. But at least a visit to the transmission security team would give her some ideas how to do it later. And maybe the night shift would be more talkative than Gary and Chris.

There was only one person on duty when she arrived. Her own office was empty; not a surprise since their job was to craft messages, not deal with emergencies.

"Hi, I'm Pen Tromarin," she said to the woman who greeted her. Pen left off her rank purposely. She wore civvies and they were probably the same rank anyway.

"Leila. Take a seat. I don't get many visitors."

Pen took a seat close to the port she wanted. "I figured it was a good idea to get to know the entire team."

"I saw your thing," Leila said. "You didn't have much real information to share."

Finally, someone who wasn't just congratulating her. "There isn't much right now. It's a big job to figure out what people need. Are you usually alone?"

"Ugh, no. My partner called in sick. He does that pretty often."

Pen saw her opportunity. "Do you get a break?"

"I don't like to take one. I keep leaving messages for

Chris to find a way for remote monitoring so I can grab a coffee or hit the head. So far no response."

"I've met Chris and Gary," Pen said. "I'll talk to them if you like."

"Really?" Leila seemed shocked. "No one cares about the night shift. Oh, sorry, that sounded like I'm complaining. Mostly it's great to be left alone. But it is hard to get things addressed, like remote access."

Leila was young and Pen felt a pang of regret that she would be tricking her. Not that Chris wouldn't get an earful tomorrow, but if anyone found the drive, Leila would be under suspicion. She had no choice though. Learning about the unauthorized communications was critical and Pen would come clean if she had to.

"Look. I can hang around if you show me what to look for," she said. "I mean, I can't do your job, but I can cover for ten minutes."

Leila looked around at the screens. Pen noticed the flow of information was only a little lighter than during the day.

"What do you think we're doing? No, scratch that. What did Gary and Chris tell you we do?"

Pen laughed. "They monitor every single data point."

"No freaking way a human can do that," Leila said, giggling.

"I let him think I believed. They have a bet, right?"

"Yeah, I heard about that. I just do my job. Look at this screen." She directed Pen to the large screen on the far wall. "See how the lines are green and yellow?"

Pen nodded.

"They're being run through a filter. It's not great because of the speed of input, but it does do a job. The green ones are either official, so don't look, administrative, so specific authorization codes, or not on the list of sketchy authorization codes. People who might be shady are automatically put in yellow status. But we still don't look at them. In the background, another program filters the messages; I don't know how. If anything comes up red, we pull it."

"What makes a message red?" Pen could guess, but Leila needed to think she couldn't guess.

"Actual flagged signatures; sender or receiver. Some trigger words in the subject line. We read them, add a flag and forward to security, and then let them go."

"So, what can I do for ten minutes?"

"Red codes don't come through very often, but we need to act fast. They get automatically shunted after we flag them. Just call me if one comes through."

Pen took Leila's contact information and settled in. As soon as she was sure the woman wouldn't return right away, Pen pulled the drive out of her pocket. What if the ports were secured? Would an alarm go out that an unauthorized device had been inserted?

If so, there would be no doubt who to blame. Pen figured she could convince the captain that it was necessary. Whitnal probably gave the drive to Asher. But Leila would be in trouble.

This opportunity was too good to pass up. She took a breath and reminded herself she had to trust Asher. If he wanted to get her in trouble, there were much easier ways.

She slid the drive into the port. No alarm. Nothing. And the drive fit flat against the casing, looking exactly like a port. It was going to be much harder to remove than place.

Ten minutes later, Leila returned, coffee in hand. "Thanks. Looks like everything is normal."

"Yep," Pen said. "Do you want me to talk to someone about your partner?"

Leila sighed and shook her head. "No, I guess he's not

that bad. They know how often he ditches. I'll let the brass decide what's best. But if you could get me a remote access, like you said, it would be easier."

Pen promised and left Leila to her job.

Before she hit her bunk to grab a couple of hours sleep, Pen received a message from the captain's aide. Orders to report to the class again and provide a presentation on the latest announcement. Pen grunted. She had far more important things to do with her time. But if that was what the captain wanted, she'd obey orders.

19

The teacher greeted her at the door to the class. "Welcome back," she said.

"Thanks. Is there some reason your class needs more information?" None of the other classes of any level had asked. Although for all Pen knew, someone else took that on.

"I thought it was a good idea to preempt their demands. I don't know why my class has become so aggressive, but I tell myself it's a good sign they're interested in civics."

Or you want me to take some of the flak for an hour.

"Any tips on specifics?" Pen had no presentation other than her announcement. If the kids couldn't or wouldn't come up with questions, she'd be back doing important work faster.

"Mellie and friends are still wound up about the transfers, but they've been quiet." The teacher drew Pen in as the class started to fill. "Try to remember these are the people who will be the future of whatever colony we build. It's hard, but they need to question things. They need to develop different skills than you or I did."

Pen glanced around the room. Mellie and her friends were clustered at the back of the room near the door. If she didn't make eye contact, perhaps other students would get a chance to jump in.

"I do remember being young," Pen said. "This experience has given me a deeper appreciation of how annoying I must have been. I was tightly focused on what I wanted and had no idea a bigger picture existed."

"Good luck," the teacher said. "Class, you remember Lieutenant Tromarin? She's here today to answer your questions." She retreated and left Pen alone, a target standing in front of a sea of pretend indifference.

"You must have questions," Pen said. "But first, let me say I'm honored to be standing here. You are the future of our colony. You have a voice, and we expect you to participate. Now who wants to go first?"

Pen carefully ignored the girls. A few hands went up. Mostly soft questions, or ones no one had the answer to. She asked the teacher to make notes, so she could answer anything left hanging.

"So, you really want to hear from us?" a boy asked. He was skinny and tall and red-haired. His face radiated interest. "Sorry, my name is Garth."

"Yes." Pen hoped he wasn't setting her up. "You can ask questions now, or you know there's a channel open. Just send a message and someone will follow through."

"Can it be anonymous?" Garth asked.

Pen hadn't thought about that. "If it needs to be, we'll set up a way. What kind of ideas do you think need to be anonymous?"

That would open up the channel to Mellie and other people like her to fill the inbox and overwhelm the process. Pen hazarded a glance and saw Mellie smile.

"I don't know. But what if people don't like what's happening? Is there going to be retaliation if someone complains?"

"There won't be any consequences, Garth. We need to hear all of it. But how am I supposed to respond if the message is anonymous?"

He glanced at Mellie and then slumped back in his seat. "That's your problem, not mine."

After a few more soft questions, Jarl put up her hand. Pen couldn't ignore her, and it was clear the girls had primed other students to ask their questions. Pen nodded to her.

"If we make it to this mystery planet, who will be in charge? Is the military still going to issue us orders?"

"Good question. The structure of the new society isn't set. Much of it depends on the planet. The civilian and military leaders are in discussions about a smooth transition from space to land. You'll notice a lot of the decisions are now coming out as joint messages." That will shut down any hints that the military is in charge of everything.

"Won't it be too late if we sit around waiting? Why isn't someone looking for public input?"

The other students muttered agreement.

Pen waited for silence before answering. She felt like some kind of specimen under observation. "That is what we are doing in this room, Jarl. And why we ask for people to send in their questions." She kept any trace of emotion out of her voice. "Public input will always be important. I'm sure you can understand that, right now, getting the fleet together and moving away is taking resources and time. You'll have plenty of opportunity to voice your opinions and ideas once we are underway."

Jarl glared at Pen and then turned to Mellie. Pen felt a

tiny bit of satisfaction. These girls were not used to being challenged.

The teacher moved to stand beside Pen. "Time for one or two more questions," she said.

"How do we know we can believe you?" Mellie asked, a sneer on her face.

"Mellie, Lieutenant Tromarin is here to answer questions, not to have her integrity questioned."

Pen took a step forward. "I said any questions were welcomed. The only answer I can give you is another question. Have I ever done anything to make you think I'm not trustworthy?"

She knew it was taking a risk. Mellie could make something up and Pen would be stuck. But it was worth it to see if she would let things go.

"We haven't had an opportunity to catch you," Mellie said.

"In that case, please give me the benefit of believing me until you have a reason not to."

Mellie huffed her annoyance and opened her pad.

"Thank you, Lieutenant. Class, prepare for the next lesson."

The teacher led Pen to the door and followed her into the hall. "I'm so sorry about those two. Something is definitely going on. I guess it's time to talk to the parents and I don't look forward to it."

"Good luck with that," Pen said. "I need to get back to my station."

PEN HAD no idea what to do next. With the drive in place, it seemed stupid to keep digging into the data. There were a few messages in her inbox, but nothing urgent. The only task she kept delaying was a wander around to listen to people. She'd had her fill of civilians, so she headed for the mess hall. Technically open to all now, it was usually only military personnel who were willing to suffer the lower variety and quality of the food.

Most of the people in the room she recognized, but only a few well enough to know their name. Liz Pernaz and Shanna Coalman stopped talking and waved her over. They'd been on the planet with the rescue team. That kind of mission made the sort of friends you could count on. Even Liz, who was pretty bent on revenge for her lover's death. Pen grabbed a coffee and joined them.

"Congrats on the promotion," Liz said. "I don't envy you."

"It's not even a promotion," Pen said, laughing. "It's hard, but I'm being assured left, right, and center that I'm the best person."

"We haven't seen you in a few days." Shanna handed Pen the sweetener.

"I've mostly been trying to get my head around the job, and how to relate to civilians."

"Is that your job? Just keeping the civilians happy?" Liz asked.

"No, but I know the military."

Shanna snorted.

"Is there something I'm missing?" Pen asked, realizing she'd taken for granted that her peers would follow orders and protocol.

Shanna tipped her head to the side. "I've only been part of your military for a few days, so maybe I'm seeing something that's not real."

"You came from Loke's ship," Pen said. "You know soldiers."

"No one is bitching, Pen," Shanna said. "That's kind of what we do, right? Grousing about orders and pretty much everything is a sport."

"No one? Yeah, it is odd. What do you think is going on?"

"Look, we follow orders," Liz said. "We aren't used to being able to actually air our views. Things are going to change when we find a planet. We all thought that would be in the future, maybe never. Now? It could happen in a couple of months. That makes people think, and makes them scared."

"What do I do?" Pen knew she couldn't just take it to the captain. Dealing with this was exactly her job.

"Remember, they need encouragement to talk to you. Hang out here a bit more," Shanna said. "Don't let us think you are only there for the civilians."

Lieutenant Tromarin, report to the captain's quarters.

The announcement caught everyone's attention. Pen stood and said, "I guess I'm in trouble. Some things stay the same."

Laughter followed her out of the mess hall.

THE CAPTAIN WAS WAITING for her, alone. Pen's stomach dropped. Her joke might not be so funny.

"You met with students?"

"Per your orders, sir."

The captain frowned at that. "Show me the orders."

He didn't remember? Pen took out her tablet and turned it to him.

"Thank you."

He didn't issue the orders. Interesting.

"You faced a few challenges," the captain continued.

"A few of the students are pushing their limits, but it was nothing I couldn't handle."

"Not everyone agrees. I will deal with it, but I thought you needed to be aware I had a call."

"From the teacher?" Pen couldn't believe she would have complained.

"It is not important who. How are you getting along with gathering input?"

"It's early days. The civilians are getting comfortable. We received a few interesting questions in the inbox, and I've had a request for public forums. It would be nice to have someone help with the volume."

"I'll see what I can arrange for you," he said. "Anything more serious?"

How to answer that? "I haven't heard anything," Pen said. "I'm following up on a few things, but nothing concrete yet."

The captain looked at her long enough that Pen wondered if he was going to order her to explain.

"I appreciate you not dumping everything in our lap, but don't leave me or Whitnal in the dark," he said. "I chose you because you are capable of independent thought. Don't make me regret it."

"No, sir." Pen was torn between getting out before she actually said something to get in trouble and lying to the captain so he wouldn't ask hard questions. Her need to do a good job won out. "I do have something."

"What?"

"I've been spending most of my time trying to find out what the civilians think," she said. "It's come to my attention that the military personnel might be feeling a bit lost."

"We can schedule a time for you to address them."

"With respect, sir, it should come from you. They need to know things aren't going to crash headlong into chaos."

The captain raised an eyebrow.

"Okay, maybe I'm being dramatic, but things are about to change completely. I think they need to know if there are plans to reduce the military complement, or increase it, or change the mandate. You don't need to give them details, they trust you. Just don't get so involved with the immediate crisis that you end up losing them."

"See? I told you I made the right decision." The captain called his aide. "Schedule time for me to walk around."

When Royce left, Pen asked, "Do I need to let you know when I am meeting with people? You called me in here because of the school visit."

"I will find out why you were ordered to go," the captain said. "You don't need to keep either of us apprised of your casual meetings. It will be sufficient if you pass on anything that we need to know about."

"Yes, sir."

"Dismissed."

20

Asher sent a message to pull the drive and meet her in the theater at the same time as before. Pulling it out was tricky, but Gary was arguing with Chris over something and she took advantage of their distraction to retrieve it.

Now she was back in her quarters trying to find a way to feel good about handing over so much confidential information. Pen figured he wouldn't miss the opportunity to set a Trojan in motion or create a back door, but she knew how to protect her terminal from anything Asher put on that drive.

She tried but she couldn't copy the drive contents. Viewing them was easy. A quick scan showed her five more fake coded communications. That had to be enough information. She highlighted the rest of the communications and tried to delete, but she didn't have the clearance needed.

"I shouldn't have agreed," she muttered. "I could have found this easily enough without risking my career."

There were official communications in the list. She could be thrown in the brig for life. Jo was right. She didn't think ahead. At least she had a few hours to figure out a solution.

Her pad pinged. *Lieutenant Tromarin, report to debrief room 3.*

The ident was from the captain's office. Had she been caught after all?

Pen closed down her terminal and slipped the drive under her mattress before hurrying out.

Debrief room 3 was only five minutes away, not long enough to worry herself into a panic, or enough to craft a decent response.

Pen stepped inside to see a man waiting. Not the captain; Wes Royce. Her fears of reprisals drained away. "Why do you want to meet me?"

He stood at ease and looked at Pen without saying a word. She got the feeling he expected her to salute. They were the same rank and Pen wasn't in the mood to pander to his ego. She smiled at him.

He didn't smile back. "You complained to the captain about having to meet with a class of students?"

"The captain heard about it. I thought he ordered me to do the visit."

"You are too familiar with the captain. Your orders don't always come from him directly."

"I should probably confirm that with him," Pen said, "unless you have some authorization to show me?"

"You need to learn protocol," he said, stepping forward and grabbing her arm.

"Let me go." It wouldn't look good for Pen to break Royce's arm, so she held onto her temper.

He increased the pressure and dragged her into his chest. "I will not let you cut me out. You will not tell the captain about this meeting. You will not question any orders that come from him."

Pen pulled away, but he twisted her arm. She should have fought back as soon as he touched her. "I report to the captain and Roger Whitnal." Her words hissed out through the pain. "I don't need them to fight my battles. Let go of me before I damage you in a way you can't hide."

He leaned closer. "Right back at you."

Pen put her right foot back to strengthen her stance and pushed forward. He grunted and pushed her away. As soon as he shifted his weight forward, Pen leaned to the side. He went down, hitting his head on the table.

"You bitch." He struggled to his feet, hand pressed on the head wound. "You will regret that."

"Are you going to tell the captain?" Pen was glad her terror didn't come out in her voice as she stepped clear of his reach. She refused to rub the pain away from her arm.

"I don't need to do that," he snarled. "I can make your life miserable without help."

"We'll see. I didn't tell him, by the way. He figured it out."

She didn't wait for a response. Time was running out for her to protect the data from Asher.

BACK IN HER QUARTERS, Pen looked at the message file again. Ignoring the trembling in her fingers, she opened one at random and tried to erase the contents. When that didn't work, she tried to scramble it. When that didn't work, she ran out of ideas.

An hour later, the only plan she felt comfortable with was adding a message of her own with a tracker. If she couldn't hide the information, at least she could find out what he did with it.

Her body finally clear of the adrenaline and fury at Royce's attack, she pulled on a long-sleeved shirt to cover the bruises that were already darkening her skin.

21

Pen went directly to the theater, no sightseeing this time. She couldn't waste time satisfying her curiosity until they knew whether the messages represented a danger or not. Later, she'd poke around until she got bored.

This time she was there first, at least the space felt empty, but the room was dark. She should have thought of that. Pen used the light from her pad to find a place to sit and keep an eye on the door.

Two minutes later, Asher slipped in and pressed a panel on the wall. "The lights are here," he said, pointing. "No one will notice the tiny drain of energy."

"How many times do you think we'll meet?" Pen didn't relish the idea of frequenting the space. Too many trips in here and you eventually attract attention. "Do we need another place?"

"We'll know soon enough." He put his terminal on a seat and held his hand out for the drive. "Let's see what we've got."

"What about the other messages?" Pen asked. "Most of

this isn't suspicious and a chunk is official. We shouldn't have access."

"You tried to erase the contents?" He smiled at her blush. "I expected you to. We'll delete everything we don't need as soon as I load it here. The drive gets wiped, and you can watch me scrub everything but the messages we need to decode."

Pen passed him the drive and watched the data load. Asher had been telling the truth. The drive was empty when the data was gone. Asher ejected it and dropped it on the floor. He smashed the casing with his heel and picked up all the pieces.

"I'll take it," Pen said. "I have a legitimate place to recycle drives at work."

"And you want to make sure I don't try to reassemble it." Asher grinned. "You would make a good spy, Pen. Don't dismiss the idea."

"Let's get this over." Pen was flattered by his comment and didn't want him to notice.

He showed her the screen. "I see you highlighted the pertinent messages."

"It was all I could do."

"Make note of a few that we don't want." Asher typed in a code after Pen nodded. She watched as the file emptied.

"Can you decode? A way not available to us mere officers?"

"Yes, but I want you to be sure I can be trusted. Try searching for any of the messages I deleted."

Pen ran queries for the three messages she'd memorized. No results. "Okay. You don't need to prove anything to me, Asher. I have to believe you because I can't stop you doing exactly what you want."

"You do have a choice, Pen. I won't put you in danger."

He reached to touch her arm and she pulled away. "Sorry. I didn't mean anything."

Trust goes both ways. As much as she wanted to keep the attack private, Pen didn't want Asher thinking she was afraid to be touched. She told him about the attack.

"What are you going to do about him?" Asher put the terminal aside. "Do you think he's involved with whatever is going on?"

Pen thought before she answered. As his aide, Royce was so close to the captain it would be easy to gather information, or anything the captain wanted kept secret. "It's hard to believe he got that position if he's secretly plotting against us."

"But not impossible, and maybe this is new for him."

"I'm pretty sure he was only defending his territory. No one, as far as I know, has had the kind of access I've been given."

"Maybe, but don't dismiss him until we have some reason to." He picked up the terminal and transferred the four files into a program. "This will take a few minutes."

"How do I gain access to that decryption?"

"You take our offer of a job." Asher kept his eyes on the screen. "I can't give you anything we use. There's a reason we keep things tightly controlled. If people found out what we could do, there would be more problems — harder ones to fix."

"I don't like knowing you have things like this." Pen wondered what other tools he had.

"We work by a strict code," Asher said. He looked away from the screen. "I promise you we don't pry into everyone's business. There are only a few of us, so we couldn't if we wanted to."

The screen filled with red text.

"It's done," Pen said.

Asher read the results. Pen couldn't make the words out without leaning in close and she wanted to hear his interpretation first.

"This is bad. This is our location and speed."

It could be innocent.

"Who is receiving the message? The scouts need that information and *Tomorrow's Promise* needs the exact coordinates to rendezvous."

"They receive it on authorized channels."

"Are you sure?"

"Yes. And if this was the scouts or the last ship, we would find a destination code."

"The messages are being broadcast to space?" That made no sense.

"Yes." Asher stared at the screen again. "Wide and deep. Like a distress beacon."

"But," Pen couldn't think what to add to the word. Why would someone send a distress signal from the fleet? "Could it be automatic? Triggered by something in the wreckage? Something's gone wrong that we haven't found out yet?"

"The auto beacon sends specific codes. These codes are fake. Manipulating them takes a human."

"Maybe there's a breach in this part of the ship." She was grasping for alternatives to avoid voicing the most probable reason.

"No way for that to happen without someone knowing, and it's not the auto beacon, Pen." Asher seemed determined to force her to state her worst fear.

"It could still be going to *Tomorrow's Promise*, or the scouts," she said. "Or a weird echo of real communications.

Yeah, I know. The faked codes and an echo wouldn't do that. Whoever is sending this wants to hide their identity, and the contents."

Asher closed the terminal. "Think it through. First, why send this?"

His question helped her calm the storm of thoughts tearing through her brain. "Are you sure there's only location and speed?"

"In these messages, yes. We need more data to be sure."

"Distress beacons are supposed to bring help." In reality no help would be close enough usually. Loke's ship had been closer than any in generations. Any farther away and they would all be dead by the time help arrived. "If not for help, then it's for homing in, right? That's what you want me to say."

"Can you really think of any other reason?" Asher kept his eyes on her. "Maybe I'm too paranoid."

Pen closed her eyes and took a deep breath. Her mind barely cleared, but a single idea floated through. "What if there are other ships? Ones we've forgotten about? Or at least most of us have?"

"And these messages are there to gather them in?" Asher didn't shut down the idea. "It's possible. We were wrong about Kalin's ship. We thought they were an alien enemy. The captain will have the answers one way or another about lost ships."

"And Whitnal," Pen said. "Will you ask him?"

"We should both ask," Asher said. "If their answers differ, we'll learn something."

That Whitnal is behind it. "But why the fake codes?" Pen asked.

"Maybe they are just old codes?"

"But why would they flag as fake? The system would recognize them."

"I don't think we can answer that." Asher glanced at his terminal. "We need more data and no matter what the reason, these communications aren't likely to stop soon."

It didn't make sense that the captain would allow the message to go out with an enemy lurking nearby. "Why would someone send a message to the enemy?" She hoped for an answer that wouldn't open more questions.

"It's hard to know what is going on in people's minds," Asher said. "Focus on what we can do. We need more information, and I think we can get it if you put in another drive."

"Like, we might learn who is sending the information?"

"I'm hoping." He took a new drive from his pocket. "We put a newer code on this one. And it will go back through the last five days."

Pen took the drive without thinking. "How would someone get a message like this out without a tag on the source terminal?"

"Easy. You've been too busy to think this through."

"I do have a real assignment." Pen was sure he didn't mean to criticize, but she felt like she'd disappointed him anyway. Her duties were as important as his spying.

He waved down her anger. "I know. You simply don't think the way we do. Up until a few days ago, the only people who communicated between ships were the captain and some of the security force. Not even Roger had access. We all just talked within the ship system."

"Yeah. And then people were transferred between ships so inter-vessel communications were opened up."

"Yeah. So, my team starts thinking we can't be sure how the other ships handled authorization. We can't be sure that all terminals are secure. Didn't one of those girls use her dad's access?"

"Are you saying some of the terminals can send long range messages? We just didn't realize that until now?"

"I'm saying we don't know. And we've never looked before. This might have been going on for a lot longer than a few days."

22

"So, what do we do?" Pen felt the gap in her knowledge keenly. It rankled that she had to learn so much when she wasn't going to join Asher, but maybe her new skills would help in her real job.

"We need to learn the signals for each ship. Maybe a list of the terminal codes. If we can figure out where the messages originated, we might be able to find the sender on one of the cameras."

"It's possible I can access some of those things, but I'm surprised you don't have clearance."

"No. Military security does, but you can't just ask them. Give me the drive back."

Pen handed the device over. "What are you going to do?"

Asher opened his terminal and inserted the drive. "I can't tell you. Try to accept the fact we can update this and gather more information."

Pen didn't respond to his assumption she would blindly trust him. She waited until he'd finished typing. Apparently the drive could be updated remotely. "If you can change the contents, why can't you do it when I've plugged it in? You would have the data and I wouldn't need to risk pulling the drive."

"It only works on a couple of terminals." He propped the terminal up and then leaned back. "This is going to take a while. I'm sorry you'll need to take the risk again. At least a couple of times."

"I'm still not okay with you gaining access to anything you want. There's a reason you need to hack in. It's supposed to be private."

"I do understand, Pen. You could simply tell the captain what you found and ask him. Why didn't you?"

"There's not enough for me to convince him," she said. "I want to give him proof first. And it's not actually in my mandate. So, if I don't give him something concrete, he might tell me to stop looking."

"Good instincts. How about I give you the permissions to delete whatever you think we shouldn't see?"

"It would help." The offer didn't completely settle her unease.

If she got caught before they found the proof, she would be in a lot of trouble. Career ending trouble. Life in the brig kind of trouble. Pen wasn't used to thinking about consequences. Her past escapades weren't such big risks.

"Next time, then. I don't want to keep asking my friend to change the code."

"How do you know what to code?"

Asher took a moment before answering. "It's something I shouldn't tell you. So, no details?"

"I can't promise I won't ask."

"I suppose that's fair enough." He checked the terminal. "This isn't new to us. Not what you found, but all kinds of little things. We found out long ago we needed more access than the military is willing to give. So, we got good at hacking."

Pen's brain popped up a handful of questions. "Why do you need me to use the drive?"

"We haven't found a way to go in remotely. We don't have access like you do." Asher didn't seem concerned. "Would you prefer we found another way?"

And then he would cut me out. "No, just curious."

He checked the terminal and then typed something. "Done." He pulled the drive and handed it to her. "This needs to be in place a couple of hours at least."

"And when will the next one be ready?" If she was running between Asher and the transmission room, she'd never get to talk to people about the changes. The fleet would be heading out today. People wouldn't leap on board with the plan to run and not fight without some encouragement.

"As quick as we can. Maybe we'll pull enough from this one. And maybe we can set the next one up to transmit to us so you don't need to retrieve it so quickly."

And that way she wouldn't be able to edit what Asher got. "Don't waste time with that."

As it turned out, Asher gave her the updated drive before she was able to insert the one she had. He asked her to leave it in place for a day. Less risk of being caught, and more data to analyze.

GARY WAS ALONE in the transmission room. Pen distracted him enough to do her job and then left for her desk. There was nothing in her inbox requiring more than a quick response. She sent a summary off to the captain, wondering if Royce would find a way to alter the contents, or delete it, to get her in trouble.

The messages in the questions and concerns box were piling up. The busy work of answering a few didn't do much to settle her nerves. Asher didn't believe Whitnal could be behind everything. She couldn't stop that very suspicion growing. Time to do a bit of investigating of her own.

She contacted Whitnal for a meeting. He said he was available right then. She wondered if that was true, or whether he would have said the same thing no matter when she called. She couldn't keep suspecting everything he did, and it didn't really matter if he was playing some game. She got her meeting.

Her cover story was getting his take on some of the questions. She made sure the list was downloaded to her pad before she left and spent the walk trying to figure out how to get him talking about what she really wanted: to trip him up and prove he was undermining the captain. The sooner she handed over the proof, the sooner she could move on with her new assignment. Or, perhaps she'd learn he wasn't conspiring at all.

"Pen, can I get you coffee?" Whitnal waved her to a seat as soon as she entered.

"I've already had more than enough today, thanks." She placed her pad on the table and took the offered chair.

"What can I do for you?" He smiled at her and took a sip of his own coffee. The office was quiet. Pen saw six desks, but no one was sitting at them.

"I sent them out," Whitnal said. "Not sure if you need privacy for our chat."

His words were reasonable, but were they true? "I have a few questions about people's concerns."

"I'm all yours."

He seemed relaxed. Pen knew it could mean he had nothing to hide, but she believed he underestimated her. She put her suspicion aside because it was distracting. She wanted to leave this meeting sure one way or another. If he was underestimating her, he would learn a lesson too.

"The one I hear most often is about how the power structure will work when we land."

"It would be nice if people only asked questions we could answer." He leaned forward and put his elbows on the table.

"Telling people it will be a transition isn't working." Pen mimicked his pose. "Everything I've learned about this job tells me that questions like this need a clear and consistent message. You, the captain, me, and anyone else who is seen as a leader must say the same thing."

"Yes."

"What is your answer? I'll craft something but I need the different views so you can sound authentic." She waited for him. If he avoided the subject and turned the conversation around every time she came to him, her job would be very difficult.

"It's good that people are confident we'll survive to land on a planet."

"Probably not what we want to open with."

He chuckled. "This is just between us. It's not like we don't have confidence; we just see the dangers more clearly."

"That's a whole other issue we need to address."

"Perhaps it's a good sign people are asking the hard questions now."

Pen sat back in her chair. If he didn't get to the point, she would just take the captain's answer. His behavior was not helping her decide to trust him.

He must have seen her impatience, because he said, "It

will be a multi-stage transition. We don't have enough information to guess how dangerous the planet is to us. We will
send military scouts first. Until a colony is established, we
will be relying on the military much as we do on the ship."

"And when the colony is established?" Pen found herself
interested despite her suspicions. "Civilians are asking
about the future, not the transition."

"We will gradually shift power to a more balanced military and civilian governance. Depending on the environment of our new home, the handover might happen quickly.
Also, if it turns out we are the only danger on the planet, the
military will slowly reduce and fulfill the policing needs. Is
that clear enough?"

"It helps." Pen made a few notes. "And the danger?
People aren't buying that this new enemy is gone."

"What can I say?" he said, shrugging. "Sometimes the
truth needs to be enough. We can only go on what we infer
from the testing, and from the scout ship reports. No one is
out there."

"Maybe we can publish some of that information in a
way the non-analysts can understand." She added that to
her list of tasks. Now it was time for her questions. "Are we
sure *Tomorrow's Promise* is the last ship?"

"Have you heard otherwise? Is that one of the
questions?"

"I'm anticipating what people don't even know they
want." She laughed. "So many of our answers are going to
be vague, it would be good to report something concrete
and maybe before someone asks the question."

"You have taken to this job. Yes, sometimes you need to
give information and not wait until it becomes an issue. We
can't look like we're not in control, right?"

Pen nodded. Why did it rankle every time someone

complemented her skills? "So, how can we be certain another ship isn't out in space?"

"We've had this discussion with the other captains and my counterparts. No one has been in contact with any other colonists. We all looked through the ancient records and can account for all the ships on the list."

"Even the ones aligned with Kalin's ship?" She didn't see any sign of prevarication in Whitnal. He was taken aback by the question. Asher hadn't briefed him.

"We should have looked for them long ago. They left after us, so we are relying on what our ancestors knew of their plans, not the actual events. All we could glean from the records was that they had four ships. Two left within a year of our exodus. The other two followed later. At least that was the plan."

"And they were all destroyed?"

"No detailed records exist from that time. When our ships left, we took the optimistic people. And the scientists. We need to talk to Kalin about this. Is he ready?"

That was a kindness she hadn't expected. "He's pretty fragile, I think. He will do his best, but he's lost. We can't wait so I suggest having someone he trusts to help."

"You? I notice you have become close."

"I was thinking something more along the lines of a counselor." She had missed the idea Kalin might have a reason for sending the messages. Had he been on the ship long enough to figure out how to create fake authority codes?

"We will make sure he is supported."

"If he says there may be another ship, what will you do?"

"I don't know. It will depend on what Kalin tells us."

"Send scouts? Broadcast a message?"

He drew back, eyes widened. "Broadcasting will only

bring trouble. No matter what we learn, we cannot let our intentions go outside the fleet."

Pen's doubts fled; that wasn't a fake. "Please don't get his hopes up if you aren't doing anything to find a ship for him to identify."

"We won't. But Kalin is not a child. And it is possible the ships settled somewhere, or just as possible they broke apart or met these new enemies."

Pen gathered her pad and stood. "I think that's all I need for today. Thank you for your time."

She could draft a few messages in her quarters. Pen was reluctant to contact the captain to meet since she had to go through Royce. Sending a draft for him to approve with a copy to Whitnal should guarantee the message was forwarded.

Her quarters were the only place she could think. When she reached her door, she stopped; it was ajar. No one had the code, not even Jo.

23

This was something the security team should deal with, but Pen wanted to know exactly what was going on before she called. She slipped her pad inside her jacket and pushed the door with her finger. No one reacted; the room was empty. The only thing out of place was a note on her table. Pen stood over it, not touching the scrap of paper. *You'll regret that. We can get to you anytime.*

Pen checked her security camera feeds. An hour ago, someone had lingered at her door. She couldn't tell who, or even if they were female or male. They were only inside for a few seconds. Not searching, just leaving the note.

She contacted the security team and stepped back into the corridor. There were too many things she'd done in the last few days that someone might not like that she had no idea what to tell the security team. It couldn't be her conversation with Whitnal, he wouldn't resort to such a juvenile threat. Her meetings with Asher? No one knew. Her digging into questions?

If Gary or Chris had found the drive, the security team would be looking for her, instead of breaking in. She sighed as she sent Asher a note letting him know. Perhaps he'd reply with an idea. Maybe she shouldn't have called the authorities.

"Tromarin?" a military police officer asked. She was dressed in the black uniform with the red stripe that denoted her position.

Pen tucked her pad away and nodded.

"Sergeant McIlroy. May I go in?"

"Nothing was disturbed," Pen said. "Only the note." She moved to follow the sergeant through the door.

"Wait here, please." She didn't check to see if Pen agreed.

Being kept out was annoying. Pen was relieved the drive was currently collecting data and she wouldn't be asked to explain why she had it or worry that the thief had access to the data.

"You can come in," McIlroy said. She was holding the note by the corner in her gloved fingers. "Are you sure this is the only thing that doesn't belong?"

"I didn't do much searching," Pen said. "My room wasn't trashed, so I figured you would want me to leave it to you."

"Good. Any idea what this is about?"

"No." Pen figured it was the truth. "I have video; where do I send it?"

"To me," McIlroy said and then provided her identity number. "Change your code. I'll authorize it to be offline. Your job might attract more people who aren't happy. At least they won't be able to unlock your quarters easily."

"Thanks. Will you keep me apprised?"

"If we find anything, yes. If you come up with a reason for this, let me know."

Pen wasn't satisfied. "Can I get a picture of the note before you take it?" Pen figured if she saw the handwriting again, it would be good to check. Although not many people used paper and pens.

McIlroy held up the paper again for Pen to photograph. "Change your code; stay safe." Then she left.

Asher replied to her message ten minutes later. *Let me see what I can find. Was there anything you don't want found?*

She responded no, and promised to check for anything that might have been left to incriminate her.

A quick search didn't uncover anything new hiding in her clothes, bed, or bathroom. She got lucky. Pen changed her code and put aside everything except crafting a message for the captain and Whitnal. One that would not mention the break in.

It took an hour, but she was satisfied with the results of her work. She needed to eat, and maybe finally talk to people about their questions.

Promising she'd go back to the mess hall later, Pen made her way to the dining hall again. Civilians needed to become used to her. And her friends hung out there more. She needed a little uncomplicated company as much as food.

As she entered, Pen found herself scanning the people for hints that they had left her the message. *Paranoia.* She was surprised at how easily her mind became suspicious.

A few people waved or nodded, acknowledging without reaching out. If this kept up, she would need to march over to strangers and initiate a conversation; not something she relished.

She ordered a bowl of soup and a glass of water and looked around. Not a friend in sight. There were plenty of empty tables. If she sat alone maybe someone would join her and tell her all their worries.

She felt guilty about being relieved when Jo showed up;

being attacked and threatened was making her antisocial. Maybe Kalin wasn't the only person needing counselling.

"It seems like forever since I saw you," he said, plunking down in the empty seat. "I guess we're both too busy to socialize."

"Is your scout training over?" She suddenly didn't want him to know about her day.

"Not even close. Those guys are trained beyond anyone else. I guess being out of the ship for days at a time means you deal with problems as they crop up."

"Or you die."

He grunted. "You sound like my instructor. I don't think I'm going to get a chance to fly."

"You can't be failing?" Jo had never failed at anything as far as Pen knew.

"Of course not, but we need experienced people out there. No one wants to risk a ship with a trainee."

"What happens if a scout can't report?" She caught herself at the last second from saying 'dies.'

"They have other trainees. Remember, I'm just getting a taste until the captain finds a permanent place for me. In a couple of days, I'm headed for the security team."

So much for keeping him in the dark. "Then you'll find out my quarters were broken into. Someone left a threatening note."

"What the hell?" Jo frowned at her. "You let me go on about training when you had that?"

"It's being handled. I didn't want you to find out by accident."

"Did you make someone mad enough to do you harm?"

Pen rolled her eyes, trying to minimize the event. "Too many to be able to pull a name I guess."

"How did they get in?" Jo wasn't going to let it go.

"They hacked my code. I changed it and it's not on the system. So I'm safe."

"Someone on this ship hacked the door code of a senior officer. Don't look at me like that, Pen. You are a senior officer by the fact of your assignment. Things are getting out of control."

"I can handle it," Pen said. "Things will settle down when we get underway. That's tonight, right?"

To Pen's relief, he didn't fight her and try to drag the topic back to the break-in. "Yes. Is the captain going to do anything to mark the occasion?"

"I haven't heard from him. But he doesn't need me for that." Pen wondered if Royce was blocking communications out of spite. She rubbed her arm as the thought brought out the ache.

"And there I was hoping for some inside scoop," Jo said, laughing.

"What are people in the training section talking about?" Pen steered the conversation to something she could control. If Jo noticed she was in pain, he wouldn't give up until she told him everything.

"I keep my head in the simulation module mostly. But all I hear is positive. People are pumped to be heading for a planet."

She wasn't naive enough to think that was all, but Jo might not realize people didn't always share fears. "Have you heard any grumbling? Anything I need to address?"

"Like someone breaking into your quarters?"

So, he hasn't let it go.

"Probably not that drastic. More like they are worried about what's happening? Or even if they are excited. It would be nice to get a positive response."

"Like I said, I've been stuck in a simulator. How are you getting your information?"

"Mostly I'm not. But that's my problem to solve."

"Pen, you're keeping something from me. Tell me and I can help."

If she did, she would never know if she was capable of doing the job without relying on him. "Some I can't tell you," she said. "The rest, I can deal with."

"Why are you shutting me out?" He kept his voice low. "Is Asher helping? Or is he causing problems? Could he be the one who hacked your code?"

Pen could understand the suspicion, but Jo needed to let things go. She wasn't going to join Asher; they were just working on this one thing. "No. He's teaching me some skills I need."

"So, he can help but I can't?" Jo drew back, hurt.

Pen pushed her empty bowl away. She didn't need this right now. "Yes. I'm sorry if that hurts, but I need him. And you need to concentrate on your training."

"He isn't your friend, Pen. He will hurt your career if he thinks it will help him."

"You don't know what you're talking about." She stood. "I need to get back to what I was doing."

"Don't be angry," Jo said. "I'm only telling you what I think. You never had a problem with that before."

"No. But things change, Jo." She left him at the table.

24

The captain still hadn't responded to her messages. Pen sat staring at her terminal, hoping to see a reply. Maybe he had more urgent things on his plate getting ready to move the fleet for the first time, but she worried that Royce was interfering.

The thought of the captain's aide made her bruises ache. She'd changed to off duty clothes since she hadn't planned any official meetings. But the tee shirt left her arms bare; something she would deal with before she went out.

It bothered her more than she expected that every action or inaction made her question loyalties. Lack of trust was the main reason she didn't even consider Asher's offer. A few days ago, she knew who to trust and life was easier.

The little voice inside undermining her logical thinking surprised her. Royce, at least, had done something to earn her suspicion. Jo? Why was she constantly on guard around him? She didn't suspect him. *But that's who will always betray you; someone with your trust.* The mean whisper came spinning from her brain.

She sat back. "No!" Saying the word out loud didn't

make anything feel more solid. The reason she was out of sorts with Jo had to do with them being separated, nothing more. That they had secrets for the first time — perhaps not secrets, but private lives. If she could share her worries with him, life would be easier.

Loke and Kalin were strangers. She wanted to trust them but needed more time. Asher? Well, she didn't trust him so no conflict there. Pen was pretty certain his helpfulness would come with a price at some point.

That's why she felt bad. Something was going on, and whatever it was threatened the ship. She couldn't talk to people about it to get a wider perspective, and the man she thought was involved clearly wasn't. That didn't make Whitnal her ally. She could only hope the data would answer some questions.

Asher might be the one you are looking for. Best place to be for him is in control of the investigation.

Pen swore at the voice.

She couldn't sit here all day. The latest update was ready to send. Departure would take precedence anyway, so it didn't matter if Royce sidelined her. She could talk to the captain. Going around his aide would be easy.

Her door chimed. Good, Jo. She would set things right.

She opened the door.

"Lieutenant Tromarin. May I come in?" The captain asked.

Pen stood aside.

"You look like you've been in the wars." He nodded to her bruises. "Trouble?"

"Nothing I can't handle, sir." She didn't want the captain stepping in and making things worse.

"I assume so, but if you need my assistance, please ask."

Pen had the creeping feeling that the captain was aware

of everything. "Will do. Did you come for a reason? I thought you'd be eyes deep in departure details."

"There is a momentary lull. It gave me a chance to follow up. I understand you met with Roger today."

She should have assumed Whitnal would bring their meeting up. "I needed his point of view on the latest civilian concerns. It's in my report."

"I haven't been paying attention to my inbox today. Brief me."

Pen gave him an abridged version of the day's report. "I wonder if we should have a separate channel for urgent communications?" This was her opportunity to cut Royce out of the equation.

"It may come to that." He looked around at the wall where Pen had stuck notes. "You had a break-in?"

"Those notes were not up then," she said. "Whoever broke in didn't learn anything." She should have asked the security officer to keep the investigation quiet. The captain had more important things to worry about.

"But you were threatened?"

"Some childish note," Pen said.

"Anything to do with the bruises?" He wasn't going to let it go so easily.

"No, sir. I'm not worried about the note. I haven't managed to annoy anyone that much as far as I remember."

"Nevertheless."

"Well, yes. Someone is annoyed."

"I won't keep you, Tromarin," he said. "You are doing good work. I know everything seems slow, but that's part of the job. I wanted two things. One is to make sure you were okay, and the other to say we have taken all military locations and codes off the database. Clearly it's not as secure as we thought."

"Thank you. I guess it's possible I'm not the only one who might be a target."

"I've asked security to keep me apprised of any other reports."

Pen didn't know what to say.

"Also, it appears my aide has been overly protective of my time. His job is to streamline my messages and he's extremely good at it. But that shouldn't get in the way of what we are doing. I will tell him your communications are a priority. We can't let Whitnal learn anything before I do." He smiled as if the comment was a joke.

"No, sir." And how would Royce take that message? Pen realized she didn't care. If she needed to keep doing an end run around him, Whitnal was her way to do it.

"Now my curiosity is satisfied, I'll return to the bridge."

"Good luck on departure."

25

Pen wandered the halls talking to anyone hanging around, but people were either busy or focused on the change. She liked assignments with more action; this waiting was driving her crazy. She joined the people in the observation room waiting to catch the first signs of movement. Someone had gone through the trouble to place scouts near each ship, reinforcing the idea that they were a fleet now, not just a ship.

"Lieutenant Tromarin?"

Pen looked around for the source of the words. Flor, one of Mellie's crew. The one girl who didn't look like she fit. Mellie and Aila were fashionable and polished. Jarl was an athlete. Flor looked like she spent more time with her terminal than a makeup mirror or sports team. "Yes."

Flor smiled slightly and then glanced around. "Can we talk somewhere for a few minutes? I promise we won't miss the start."

"Outside." Pen led her to the other side of the entrance. No one lingered in the corridor because everyone in this section of the ship was glued to a screen. "What can I do for you?"

"Um, I guess I want to tell you I don't like what Mellie and the others are doing."

A little bullying wasn't a problem for Pen, but Flor seemed more worried than that. "What are they doing?"

"I can't tell you here," Flor said. "Someone will see us talking and it will be bad for me."

Was Flor part of the group simply so they would have someone to push around? It explained why she felt so bad about their behavior. "There's no one here," Pen said. "Mellie doesn't bother me. Is she bullying you?"

"Please, meet me later."

It would be nice to shut down the little gang. If anything got Flor out of their clutches it would be a bonus. And Pen had nothing else to do until she and Asher checked the data on the drive.

"Okay. Where should we meet?" She wasn't going to let the girl into her quarters.

"There's a place I go when I need to think," Flor said. "Please don't tell anyone."

"Is it dangerous?" Pen would not keep a secret that put Flor in peril.

She shook her head. "Not really. It's in the abandoned section. I think it used to be a maintenance room, but it's big and quiet and no one else goes there."

She would be surprised. "When?"

"In a couple of hours. I need to watch the departure with my friends and then I can slip away."

"Okay. Give me the directions and I'll meet you."

Pen made a note of the location as Flor slipped back into the room. Pen closed her pad as the chime signaling the start of their departure rang. She slipped back into the observation lounge. The stars were shifting position slowly. From this perspective, the sight was beautiful as all ships turned and pointed in the same direction. Pen scanned the room. Flor was sitting just to the side of the other girls.

PEN SLIPPED through the door to the abandoned section two hours after the ship departed the wreckage site. She'd gone looking for Kalin earlier with no luck. She figured that leaving his shipmates behind, even just their corpses, would be as hard as hearing about their fate. He apparently wanted privacy, so she would let him have it for now.

The meeting place was in the opposite direction of the theater, and much deeper into the section than Pen had been before. She wondered how many other people used the abandoned rooms for secret meetings. Not too many, otherwise Asher wouldn't feel safe.

The deeper she went, the more the area declined. Dust smeared the wall where a mech's fan had passed. A spider web or two draped the dark corners. The ship carried a full complement of Earth's lost flora and fauna. Spiders had escaped early, going after the flies that couldn't be contained in the gardens. The sound of a motor running behind her made Pen turn: a maintenance bot scanning the walls.

Maintenance was carried out to ensure the ship remained safe, and cleaning would only take a couple of days when they needed room to expand. These thoughts didn't make Pen less twitchy as she turned another corner following Flor's directions. How had she found a private place so far in? And why couldn't she use any of the empty rooms Pen passed?

Twenty minutes after she entered the abandoned area, Pen reached the door Flor described. It was a darker gray than the others. A worn-out plaque hung on the wall beside it that might have read 'Maintenance' in the past but could have easily read 'men's locker room.'

She pulled the door and stepped into the darkness. Pen patted the walls for a light switch while holding the door ajar with her foot. When she found one it only turned on a faint bulb over the door. This wasn't a maintenance room. The space was too big and too crowded with equipment for that. It was a machine shop. Where teams repaired mechs or took them apart for salvage. This couldn't be Flor's safe place.

Pen turned to leave. She would work her way back to the entrance while she messaged Flor for the right location.

A shifting noise stopped her before she touched the light switch. Something being dragged. In the back, behind some equipment.

It was too late to hide her presence, so Pen walked down the center of the room between what looked like welding equipment on one side and giant bins of parts on the other.

The sound didn't repeat.

Pen kept moving forward. If Flor was in trouble, she couldn't leave. She slid her hand into her pocket to wake up her pad. She was wearing her off-duty clothes and that meant no weapon, but she could record whatever happened.

As she passed the last machine lurking in the shadows created by the weak light, Pen saw the toe of a shoe. She ran toward it. "Flor?"

No one answered.

When she got closer, Pen saw it was the casing of a mech caster, not a shoe. She pulled her pad from her pocket and activated the flashlight, shining the beam into the dark corners. There were no footprints. Not even wheel marks in the dust to explain the noise.

It came again. From a recess at the back of the machine. Pen stepped forward, shining the flashlight ahead. An operator cage sat at the end of the machine. Not one for a mech, for a human. She shone her light around the ceiling. It was covered in broken light fixtures. Pen struggled to think of a natural explanation, but it was clear someone had broken them.

She checked and the cage was empty, but the sound came again. Pen moved closer and listened, trying to keep her attention on everything.

A valve raised open and the sound came again. This time air moved against her cheek. The life support system needed a cleaning. Pen laughed in relief. No one was lurking. Flor wasn't dead.

She sent her message to Flor as she retraced her steps to the door. If the girl wanted to talk, they'd find another time, and a place closer to civilization.

The sound came again as she hit send. Clearly a breathing noise, not a body being dragged. Her imagination was too active.

A sharp pain stung the back of her head, her knees gave way, and Pen sank into darkness.

26

Pen opened her eyes.

She was on the floor, rolled to her right side. Someone had tied her hands behind her back. Her knees and ankles were also restrained. Her pad lay smashed on the tiles just beyond her shoulder.

She was in a different room. By the way her shoulders ached, she'd been dragged here. Rolling onto her back, Pen ignored the added pain. She couldn't stand up until her legs were free.

This had been someone's quarters. Just an empty room now. No one was with her.

Whoever had brought her here didn't know the right way to restrain someone. Pen wiggled her wrists and felt ease in the knots. She'd end up with abrasions, but freedom was worth the damage.

I should never have come here without telling anyone. That will not happen again.

Her wrists started bleeding, but it helped to grease the rope. Pen slipped one hand out and then shook the restraint off the other before sitting. A wave of nausea and vertigo sent her back to the floor. Her wrists weren't the only part of her bleeding. Pen touched the sore spot on the back of her head; a complication she didn't need.

Pen rolled back onto her side and drew her legs up. Untying her knees helped, but she couldn't reach her ankles. If her attacker came back, she was lost.

She pushed herself into a sitting position supported by the wall. This time the vertigo was milder. She took a breath and reached down to her feet. Getting free took longer than she hoped, but her feet were finally clear.

No way she could hide these injuries like the bruises.

If her pad was still active, she could call someone. Asher. She would call him. He could trace her location and bring help.

Asher would know what to do.

It was going to be impossible to stand and then reach down for her pad. Pen tried to grab it without falling over, but her fingers fell a few centimeters short. The pounding in her head was like a clock ticking down. Her captors wouldn't leave her alone long; they'd be back soon. She saw only one option.

Pen slid down to lie on the floor again and inched her body forward until she reached the pad: dead. But someone might be able to salvage the memory.

So, one step at a time. Could she stand?

She wiggled back to the wall and pushed until she stood upright. Her head pounded even more, but the vertigo was absent. Pen placed her palm against the wall and took a step away. Dizzy but not completely falling down. She took another step and let go of the wall. If she kept her eyes on a point ahead, she would manage.

Pen pulled the cuffs of her jacket down to cover the damage on her wrists. The blood on her clothes looked like dark patches on the black. It was hard to think, and every second she stayed in the room, the risk of discovery increased.

The theater comm units were the only ones within reach. If she got there, she could fix up something. She had to keep this as quiet as possible. If her attacker was the only one who knew about it, she would be able to identify them. If Mellie and her gang had attacked her, the problem would end with them in the brig. If it wasn't them, she didn't have any idea who.

Pen took another cautious step. She could do this. Not fast, but at least she would be out.

The door slid open without any resistance. Pen held onto the frame as she leaned forward to scan the passage-way. Not a good idea; a wave of dizziness almost floored her. No one was there. She stepped out and placed her hand against the bulkhead. She was still in the abandoned section with no indication of exactly where.

The passageway was clean, so she wasn't too far in. Since she already faced to the left, Pen started walking, each step tentative, waiting for the vertigo to tumble her world.

At the end of the passageway, she took a breath and leaned around again. The dizziness was less overwhelming. The theater doors were only ten meters away.

It took longer than Pen hoped to get inside the safety of the theater. Her equilibrium improved as she went, but she was careful not to get cocky.

Inside she made it to the comm unit: active. Asher's doing? She didn't care. He answered the comm as soon as the call connected. Pen told him what she knew. He told her he'd be there fast.

Pen looked at the seats only a few meters away, but it was an open space. She would never make it. She leaned against the wall and slid to the floor.

27

"Pen."

The word dragged her to consciousness. She opened her eyes; Asher was leaning over her and a woman was hovering behind. "Yeah."

"This is Sheila. She's a medic who knows how to keep a secret."

When Pen struggled to stand, Asher pressed her down. "We'll move you. Just let us do the work."

She couldn't deny how helpless she was, but between them, Asher and Sheila guided her to a seat. Asher stepped back and let the medic examine her.

"I'm going to scan your head," she said. "We'll look at the other wounds as soon as we know what's going on there."

Pen kept her eyes open, afraid she would pass out if she didn't. Sheila passed a probe over the damage and made a reassuring noise. All medics did that. Then she cleaned and bound Pen's wrists.

"Any other problems?"

"No. What's the deal with my brain?"

"You're lucky. No concussion. The dizziness will pass

soon. It's the adrenalin and related hormones. Drink water, and rest. You'll be fine." She pulled a bottle of water from her bag and two pills. "These will help with the pain. Let me seal the wound and you can clean up. No one will find out unless you tell them."

"Thanks." Pen popped the pills in her mouth and chugged the water.

Sheila sprayed sealant on the head wound and tested it for gaps. "Okay. I need to tell you to get checked out, but I know you won't. If you continue to feel dizzy after an hour or so, call for help, no excuses. If you get double vision, go for help. If you don't, you will die. I'm not kidding."

"But you said..."

"Pen. The scan isn't foolproof. You could have a hidden bleed. Either of those symptoms mean we missed something. Don't wait, don't explain. Call a medic and lie down if either of them happens."

"Fine. I promise." Pen hoped she wouldn't experience either. It felt like the attack meant they were close to finding out what was going on. She didn't want to miss anything because she was dead.

Sheila gave Asher more instructions and then left them to talk.

"You should have called me before going."

Pen shook her head, instantly regretting the move. "I didn't think it was a problem. A girl asked me for help. One of the teenagers I've been butting heads with."

"And she needed to meet with you in a deserted part of the ship? At night? When you might not be missed for hours?"

She didn't have the energy to argue, or even point out the contradiction that Asher used the theater for privacy. "Looking back, it was a stupid move," she mumbled.

"Jo would kill me if you disappeared."

"Not your fault."

"He would still blame me."

"I really need some rest, Asher. Can we leave the lecture until tomorrow?"

"You need to tell the captain what happened."

"When I know for sure who it was," Pen said. "I'll be fine when he needs me."

"No. You need to tell him because I'm going to report this to Whitnal."

And Whitnal would blab to the captain.

"Okay, after a few hours' sleep. I promise."

He sat beside her. "I'll give you that. What makes you think it's not these teenagers?"

"It might be. But it's hard to believe they are behind these communications. They're kids."

"Did you check your messages? If it wasn't them, this girl should be trying to find out why you stood her up."

Pen pulled her damaged pad from her pocket. "Not possible until I get back to my quarters."

"You think someone followed you?" Asher asked. "I mean, if it wasn't her, how did the attacker know where you would be?"

"Maybe I stumbled in on something. Maybe that's why I was left so close to the entrance."

"And she gave you the wrong directions?"

"Maybe. I don't know, Asher. I can't think this out right now. I need my bed."

"I'm staying with you," he said. "No arguments. I'll hook you up to the med scanner and watch for problems."

"How long have I been gone? I don't want to face people's assumptions if you are in my quarters overnight."

"Five hours since the fleet headed out."

"Then no one has missed us yet. And it's too late to call Flor."

"If she isn't bombarding you with messages about not meeting her, no."

"Fine. Can we go?"

Asher helped her stand and supported her to walk. "If it wasn't just you stumbling onto someone's secret, we're getting close."

"I figured, but why is it me that has to get hurt?"

WHEN PEN FINALLY WOKE, she was alone. On her desk was a new pad with a note from Asher attached: *Keep this one safe.*

Nothing from Flor.

Pen showered and checked the seal on her wounds. Her wrists were fine, but her head needed to be covered. Civvies again. She tucked her pad into her pocket, swallowed two painkillers and headed out. There was no school today so the girls might be a bit hard to find. Pen headed for the dining hall. She needed some food and maybe Flor would be there.

The corridors were busy. Apparently, a lot of people had business now that the fleet was traveling. Good. With something to occupy their minds, there would be little for her to deal with. The next couple of days promised to be hard on her physically.

Pen headed for the counter to order a breakfast sandwich before scanning the room. Luck was with her. The little gang sat at a corner table. And none of her friends were around to notice the damage to her head.

She ordered her sandwich to go so she could confront the girls and then leave.

As she approached the table, Flor's face went bright

red. She probably didn't want the others to find out about their conversation. Too bad. Pen had followed Flor's directions. The girl had made a mistake or sent her to be attacked.

"Flor, what happened to you last night?" No need to be tactful.

"What do you mean?"

Mellie glanced between Pen and Flor. "Why are you harassing us?"

Pen didn't look away. "I'm talking to Flor."

"Then why are you harassing her? My father can complain, you know." Mellie still thought she had some weight to throw around.

"We were supposed to meet," Pen said. "You didn't show."

"No," Flor said. "You never came. I waited for an hour and you never showed up."

"Why were you meeting her?" Mellie asked Pen. "Is that appropriate?"

Pen ignored her. Flor's color had faded, and she looked like she was about to pass out. Was she too afraid to admit she wanted out of the group?

"Flor, you gave me directions. I went there."

Mellie shoved her chair back and stood. "Why were you meeting her? You can't just demand we come to you. It's not safe there."

How did Mellie know the meeting was in the abandoned area? "Flor asked for the meeting. You can ask her for details." There was something more going on here. The most benign reason was that she knew where Flor hung out. But it was highly possible that they set her up.

"I am not your enemy, Mellie." Pen wanted the attacks to stop. "You don't need to threaten me or try to hurt me." Pen had her suspicions confirmed when Mellie smiled. She turned and walked away.

In the corridor, she heard someone running toward her. Pen turned, ready to fight. Flor stood behind her, head down.

"I'm sorry. Whatever happened last night, we didn't have anything to do with it. I waited, like I said. Mellie didn't know; none of them did. I told her I was going to tell you to back off when I talked to you. They didn't know I was asking you to meet me. Please don't tell her I was going to give you secrets."

Flor was a lousy liar.

"Just leave me alone. I have too much to do to play these stupid games. If your behavior continues, I'll give your name to security for the investigation into who broke into my quarters."

Flor's eyes blazed. "You wouldn't dare. My parents aren't important like theirs. But I am still protected. Tell security and you'll regret it."

She turned and ran back to her friends.

Pen kept walking to the transmission control room. It was time to pull the drive. If she had any proof that the break-in was committed by one of those teenagers, she'd tell Sergeant McIlroy in a heartbeat.

When Pen stepped through the door to the transmission control room, Gary was standing in front of the drive. He was looking at the bank of servers. Pen held her breath, waiting for him to turn around and accuse her.

He didn't.

"Hey, guys," she said as casually as she could. "Find anything interesting since we've moved?"

Gary turned. "No. I'm beginning to think our bet is never going to be collectable. That or Janice is not doing a great job of judging." He returned to his seat. "Can I do anything for you?"

Adrenalin buzzed through Pen's veins. It took an effort to speak normally. "I thought I'd sit and watch for a while. It's going to be a few days before I need to do any work."

Chris turned from the screen. "Not much right now. Mostly ships tweaking their position. If you are going to hang out, I can go get us coffee." He stood and offered his seat.

Not close enough for Pen to reach for the drive. "Thanks." She would need to find a way to make Gary leave, too.

She watched the screens for a few minutes before asking, "How do you know what's in the communications?"

"We don't, but the codes give us a hint on official ones." He pointed to the screen, following a line that jerked down as new communications filled the top. "This code is navigation. This one is engineering."

"I would be bored sitting and watching this all day." She shifted in her seat. "Do you get bathroom breaks? Or are you scared Chris will find something when you are gone?" She laughed as she said the words.

"The head isn't that far," Gary said. "In fact, I'll hit it when Chris gets back. Coffee makes me go, if you know what I mean."

"I can make sure no one comes in if you want to go now." All she needed was a second to pull the drive. "That way he'll be at a disadvantage, right? Missing more of the message stream?"

"I shouldn't leave you alone."

"I have the clearance, Gary. I promise no one will find

out. I've done it before." Pen sent a silent prayer to whoever ruled chance that he'd bite. "What's two minutes?"

She could see Gary think it over. He had to go now, or Chris would be back.

"No, I'm good." He settled back in his chair. "What did you mean you've done it before?"

"Oops," Pen said with a grin. "I can't tell." She turned to look at the screens again.

"How is your job going?" Gary asked. "I saw the announcement, everyone did."

"Still trying to get a handle on everything," Pen admitted. "People are reluctant to talk to me. And the messages coming in are easy questions. I know there's more, but I guess I need to make a few more relationships before I gain trust."

Gary nodded and checked the time.

"Chris is taking a while," Pen said. "He's not as worried as you about missing something."

"He's probably chatting. Yeah, I guess the bet is mostly my idea."

"You have to do something to spice up your day," Pen said. "I've had my share of misadventures doing that."

"I thought you hard duty types were always involved in the interesting assignments."

"Not until the rescue. Before that, most of the time we train and run simulations." Pen kept her eyes on the screen as she talked. "Do you need to watch the screens your whole shift?"

Gary shrugged. "No. But there's not much else to do. If the system flags something, we'll see it."

"So why do you?" Pen looked around the room. Gary was right, there didn't seem to be much beyond the message streams.

"We can't do anything distracting. Chris isn't exactly a brilliant conversationalist, so I watch."

And the system doesn't flag much, Pen thought. "How long do you think Chris will be?"

"Who knows? He doesn't talk much here, but if someone got him on the latest flash hockey scores he'll talk forever." Gary shifted in his seat.

"I guess I should go find something more interesting to do if you don't mind waiting for him."

"Before you go, could you watch the screens for two minutes?"

"Go ahead," Pen said. "I can cover. Just don't be long."

Gary hurried out.

Pen reached for the drive. It popped into her hand.

"What's going on?" Chris asked. He stood at the door holding two coffees.

"Nothing," Pen said. "Gary will be right back."

"He shouldn't have left you."

Pen stood to give Chris his seat. "He's been gone less than a minute."

"He still should have waited." Chris looked around. "You aren't part of the team."

"Sorry." Pen saw no benefit in arguing. This was the last time Asher would talk her into something that she couldn't do in the open. Her pad pinged. A summons to the captain's briefing room. "I'll see you around."

She left Chris grumbling and staring at the screen.

28

"I see you've taken to camouflage," the captain said when Pen entered.

If he made her take off the hat, she wouldn't be able to hide the wound on her head. "Sorry, sir. It seems to put civilians at ease, or at least not quite so on guard."

"I leave it to you. But perhaps your formal appearances could be in uniform." He indicated she should sit. "We have some details on our potential home. We expect to broadcast soon but haven't set a time yet."

That should answer a raft of questions.

Until she and Asher managed to find out what was going on with the messages, Pen worried about disclosing anything the captain wanted to keep safe. If someone was trying to bring the enemy close — although why was a complete mystery — knowing the destination would be disastrous.

"So, we've identified a specific planet?" Pen asked, keeping her worries to herself.

"A system, at least. We've had a general direction from

the moment we lifted off Earth, but the original plan antici-
pated it would take generations."

"I think most people believe we were wandering," Pen
said. "Why didn't we explain the purpose long ago?"

"The enemy. The one we now know as Kalin's group.
They attacked early. The original fleet captains decided to
keep certain things secret for the survival of the human race.
They obfuscated so much; we didn't look for anything below
the surface. All the captains had orders to make for the
same section of space, but we drifted apart to minimize the
opportunity to wipe us out."

How much death could have been avoided if the truth
wasn't hidden? "And now we gained another enemy," Pen
said. "One that can't possibly be human in origin."

"Let us hope we've lost them. It is possible they know
nothing of our ships." The captain pulled up a star map and
zoomed in. "Here is the system. I've arranged for you to
access the details, just not the specific location."

Pen thought it was an excellent idea. "That information
is secure, right, sir?"

"No one can find it." He glanced at her as if about to ask
why she worried about security. He didn't. "We feel it is
better if no one starts researching and staking claims."

"We?"

"The captains and civilian leaders."

"What information would someone find if they did get
through the protections?" Pen struggled to imagine how
someone would know enough to stake a worthwhile claim.

"There's data from probes. We don't know how reliable it
is. They didn't get close enough to look for human-eating
trees." He chuckled.

Would it make a difference if they were united? That was
a question for later. It was enough she had something to

share and time to worry about the details later when they knew it was safe. "What do we know, sir? That we can share."

"The distance from the sun is optimal for two of the planets. Scouts are ready to go ahead of us when we get close enough. Right now, we need them protecting our perimeter."

"How long before the scouts can send back something more concrete? The last planet I stood on looked friendly until the trees started to murder us."

"People have the details about your rescue mission, Pen. Do you think they heard enough to worry about that kind of danger?"

"Enough, yes. But even if they didn't, Loke's survivors might start talking as soon as we announce anything."

"Take care of that in any announcements then." The captain turned back to the screen. "We have not yet decided which of the planets to attempt first."

Pen looked at the image. The system was comprised of twelve planets. Two giants with multiple large moons. All but two of the planets faded into the background, highlighting their options. "Any of the moons viable?"

"We will get that information from the scouts," the captain said. "We only have enough resources to colonize one of the planets. If we need more detail to pick our home when we approach, we'll send an advance team to explore both. But we will only colonize one. We'll leave expanding to future generations."

"I need this image," Pen said. "Have someone remove or scramble the stars first. I don't want any amateur navigators figuring out the location."

"I'll have it sent today." He turned his attention to Pen. "Send me a plan by end of shift."

"Yes, sir." Pen looked down at her pad, not wanting to meet the captain's gaze. She didn't have black eyes, but he might notice the effect of her pounding headache and ask for a reason. If he did, she wouldn't be able to lie. The discussion of secrets had already made her want to disclose what she and Asher found.

"Have there been any further attempts to enter your quarters?" he asked.

"No, sir. I think the new security level is working."

"I trust you will advise me if something happens I should know about." He sounded concerned and suspicious. Perhaps this was his way of telling her he trusted her to make the right decision.

"Yes, sir."

"Very well, lieutenant. Dismissed."

Pen picked up her pad, stood, and saluted.

Relief at not having to tell the captain about the attack, and as she feared, revealing everything she held back, loosened the pain in her head. And spending time creating some good news was better than any painkiller. The drive was burning a hole in her pocket, but without Asher she had no hope of deciphering the contents. Was it foolish to hope they had nothing more to investigate?

Tired of her quarters but worried the dining hall was too public for her, Pen needed somewhere else to work. A place where she didn't run the risk of bumping into her friends. Jo would know right away something was wrong.

The other options didn't look great either. Working at her desk depressed her because she felt more isolated seeing the team work together. Maybe her head injury magnified the feeling, but it was real. If she worked in the mess, it meant comments about her civvies. The thought of slipping into the abandoned area made her queasy.

The observation lounge. The light was dimmer, fewer people hung out in the gloom, none of her friends at least. Kalin might, but he had no reason now that they were far from the wreckage. Pen changed direction and a bit of her anxiety slipped away.

Asher was making his way toward her; that changed her priorities. They could review the stolen data and maybe end their investigation. She smiled at him. He didn't respond and kept walking past her. Why?

Pen turned to watch him go and noticed Jo at the end of the corridor. She waved and he hurried off. Did Asher know how Jo felt about his work? It didn't matter; she didn't have the strength for another argument, or for putting on a brave front. The observation room waited.

Only a few steps later a voice interrupted her concentration. "I thought you'd stay away from us."

Mellie! Another thing Pen didn't have the strength for. "It's a public space."

"Convenient," Mellie said. "I liked it when we were separated. At least then we had some privacy."

Pen couldn't think of a response, or one polite enough not to get her in trouble. She simply walked away. She'd had enough of them. They needed a lesson in how to live on a ship. Not from Pen, but she'd take the time to talk to Whitnal. He was the civilian leader, time for him to start leading.

29

Now she was more irritated than excited. Her head pounded and she'd left the painkillers in her room. The thought of going back just to pick up the pills was too much. The headache would subside. She couldn't let Mellie and her little gang rule her day. They might have set her up for the attack, but there was no proof. Pen had a message to create and a meeting with Asher to get to. The observation lounge was still her best choice. And she could have tea there to help with the pain.

As she walked into the small vestibule containing dispensers for snacks and beverages, Pen's pad pinged. She ignored it for the time it took her to order a tea from the machine. Nothing could be that urgent.

She took a sip and grimaced at the flavor. Herbal tea might be gentler on her system, but pills didn't taste like boiled garbage.

The message was from Kalin. He was in the observation room and wanted to meet her. Pen took her tea and went into the room proper. Now that she had a concrete task, the universe seemed to be determined to keep her from starting. But Kalin hurt now and she couldn't put him off.

He was waiting in the center of the room, facing the screens. He looked so alone. There were only two other groups of people and they were huddled over their conversations, separated from Kalin by the width of the room. On purpose? Did people shun him?

"Hey," she said, sitting beside him.

"Thanks for coming," Kalin said. "I haven't seen you for a while."

"Busy. How are you?"

He sat up and leaned toward her. "Better because of you. Making me talk to a professional helped... is helping."

"I'm glad." Pen touched his shoulder. His words lightened her mood. Not everyone always sniped at her or tried to stop her from exploring new things like investigating a serious mystery. Here was someone she'd actually helped.

"What's wrong?" Kalin's question broke through Pen's self-congratulations.

"Nothing."

He shook his head. "You didn't let me get away with that answer. You're hurt."

Pen reached to touch her neck, thinking that her wound was bleeding, but her fingers came away dry. "What makes you think that?" Pen needed time to make up a story.

"You touched your neck when I asked, so don't pretend."

"But that was after."

"You are holding yourself stiffly. I'm used to assessing injuries to my unit. It's obvious if you know what to look for."

"So, everyone can tell?" The captain had been hinting. Good thing Jo didn't come closer earlier.

"Not unless they have the same training. What happened?"

Pen almost blurted out the whole story but kept silent because she didn't want Kalin to rush out to defend her. Or try to find out who did it. "Nothing I can talk about."

"Didn't you tell me that it's not good to keep things inside?" He laughed at her expression. "Don't worry. I'm not as pushy as you. If you want to keep secrets, I'll honor it. But you do need to stop holding yourself so tightly. First, you can't hide it from people for long, and second, you will not heal properly. Move your shoulders and neck."

Pen rolled her shoulders and noticed how tight they were. Moving her neck was a different project. Fear of a dizzy spell kept her stiff. She put her hands on the arms of the chair first to avoid tipping over if vertigo overwhelmed her balance.

"That's right, just looking left and right will do it. In your quarters, you should roll your neck."

Pen gave a tight nod. The ship didn't tilt, so maybe she was fine. "Thanks. Look, I have some work to do now, but we should get dinner. We all should."

Kalin stood. "Yes. I think we need to work on keeping our friendship going. I expect to be assigned to a job soon, and none of us is easily available."

He left her to her job.

Pen settled back in the soft chair, her pad on her knees. Careful to move her head occasionally, she created a communication plan while she waited for Asher to arrange their next meeting. The pleasure of preparing good news was shadowed by the fear of what those messages contained.

30

I t didn't take long for Asher to ping her with a time for the meeting. She went back to her quarters after sending her plan for publishing the new information off to Whitnal and the captain. The tea had only softened the pain; she needed the pills to be alert this evening.

Taking Kalin's advice, Pen exercised her neck. No vertigo, so she was healing. If she kept that in mind, maybe she wouldn't try to keep her head immobile when she was out.

The wounds on her wrists were healing nicely, but the bruises left by Royce on her arm were only now getting colorful. If the events of the first couple of days of her new assignment set an example of how it would be, she wouldn't last long.

This time she wasn't going to the abandoned area unprepared. Along with the drive, Pen carried a flashlight large enough to be used as a weapon. She set her pad to record. If anyone attacked, at least there would be an audio recording. The blank space in her memory just before blacking out was worrisome.

Thankfully, they were meeting in the evening this time.

No need to be up until all hours. And some hope of getting a night's sleep after.

"How's the head?" Asher asked.

"Painful. Kalin figured it out." She dropped into a chair beside him, pulling out the drive and handing it to Asher. "I'll live as long as I don't get another whack."

"What did Kalin figure out?" Asher asked quietly.

"Not what happened. Just that something did. I'm not sure how long it will be before Jo or Loke realize I'm not a hundred percent. I've kind of avoided people I know as much as possible."

"You met with the captain." Not a question.

"Do you have me tagged?" She tried to make it a joke but all the frustration of the last while seemed to slide out with the words.

"No, but maybe I should." Asher laughed, either not bothered or understanding how much the injury was getting in the way of her normal mood.

"Then you can find me if I'm killed," she said. "I might volunteer to be tagged."

"Roger told me about the meeting. You have some good news, right?"

How much did he tell Whitnal? "Yeah. Does Whitnal know about the messages? I haven't told the captain."

"No. But we can't keep this quiet much longer. I'm happy to be there when you explain if you want." He pulled a device from his pocket.

"Oh, sure, I get all the flak for keeping secrets."

"I will happily step in when they realize we did the right thing."

Pen grunted a laugh. "What's that?"

He showed it to her. A black plastic box about ten centimeters on each side and only a few thick. One port and a small screen. "This will read the data and with luck give us some answers."

Answers would be nice. "Are we totally sure that these aren't going to scouts? They do need to know how to return to the ships."

"I will be surprised if that is the answer." Asher inserted the drive into the port. "Scouts use their own codes. Even if the other ships use different ones, they wouldn't be false."

"Could these be coming from another ship? Why would they be in our transmission stream?"

Asher put the device on the seat beside him. "If it was me, I'd do my best to disguise the origin point. Whoever is doing this might be relaying through us. It's never been possible to do that before."

"And if it turns out to be from another ship?" Pen couldn't imagine the captain sending anyone out to investigate.

"That's not our problem, unless your captain and Roger make it so."

Pen glanced at the device. Nothing flickered; it looked inactive. "What do you want the answer to be?"

Asher looked at her with a frown. "It only matters what it is, Pen."

She huffed. "I know, but I'm hoping for something innocent. I don't want to find out someone is betraying the whole fleet. All of humanity? Why would anyone do that?"

"I don't want it to be that either, Pen. I'm not hungry for a plot here. But people do things for all kinds of reasons."

"Like they don't want to live to be part of the future and think no one else should?" She couldn't wrap her mind around it. Even Kalin didn't want to kill everyone, and his own people were all dead.

"How well do you remember your Earth lore?"

"Nothing more than the basic. Why we left and... I guess that's it."

Asher nodded slowly. "I guess the civilian side is more interested. We get a bunch of the history. Probably because we are supposed to learn how not to do things like make war because we disagree on something."

"That didn't work out. We've been at war with Kalin's group."

"Yes, see how hard it is to change our nature?" Asher glanced at the device and then back to her. "We get along on the ship. Mostly because we need each other to survive. We can't just kill off a bunch of people and take over. Too many specialized tasks."

"But that wasn't true on Earth. And it won't be true on the planet soon enough." A whole new raft of problems waited for them in the future.

"Yes. There were people who thought they could save everyone through death. That there was a better world waiting. Or people who thought they owned their families. Or people who just lost the ability to care. Imagine what would have happened if one of the religious cults who killed everyone to help them to a higher plane tried that on a ship?"

Everyone would be dead.

"So, we got rid of the beliefs?"

"No. The situation meant people cooperated. No one slipped into the mental state that gave them the idea. If anyone gets depressed or starts acting odd, someone gets them to a counselor. We have to."

"But now people are focused on what's happening, not

on everyday life?" Pen knew it wasn't quite the right idea, but she couldn't imagine life any different.

"Yes. And anyone who has the tendencies toward annihilation can slip by without someone noticing."

"We can't keep this a secret. If you're right, it's too dangerous." Pen stared at the device, willing it to beep or ping or light up with answers.

"It could also be something innocent like someone reaching out to a lover on a scout ship," Asher said.

"Can we block the signal?" Pen didn't like the fact that the broadcast was still going out.

"Then they'll find another way. And we might not notice it soon enough."

"You think they are monitoring?" If this person knew Pen and Asher were interfering, it would explain the attack.

"We can't take the risk."

"Can we send our own messages?"

"You mean to confuse someone?" He shrugged. "Maybe. But it will be a distraction."

"Fine, we'll focus on the perpetrator for now."

A light flashed on the screen of the device.

31

A sher removed the drive and destroyed it just like the last one. Pen pocketed the pieces for the recycle chute. "What does it say?"

"Just give me a second." Asher placed the drive next to his terminal and linked them through the system net.

"Is it safe?" she asked. And then when he looked at her sideways, she laughed. "Okay. I guess you made sure."

He typed a few commands and Pen looked over his shoulder at the results. Twenty-five messages rose from the background data. "This is all of them," he said.

"Is that right?" she pointed to the date column. The messages had been going out for a week. Since Kalin and Loke's shipmates had arrived.

"Yes. Suspicious, but not proof." He typed again. The background data disappeared. The remaining messages aligned on a timeline. "So mostly late at night, but not all."

"What did the device do?" Pen asked. "We had this information from before." The fact there were more of them was because the messages continued to be sent, not that it found different ones.

"The device stripped out the code. We should be able to read the contents. You want to start at the beginning or the end?"

"They are all about the same size, so I don't think it matters much."

Asher opened the first message.

All it contained were the ship's coordinates. Each of them contained that information. The ones from today were different. The coordinates with direction and velocity.

"It's enough for the recipient to locate and track us," Pen said in a whisper. "There's no innocent interpretation."

"Not one we can think of, but the sender might have a good reason." Asher didn't sound convinced.

"Is it being received?" Pen asked. There were no responses, but maybe Asher had attached tracers. "Where is it coming from?"

"It's just being broadcast," he said. "No way of knowing if someone is listening unless they respond."

"Or show up near the scouts, or attack," Pen added. "It could be an invitation to join the fleet, or to come attack us."

"Let's hope we get more warning than Kalin's people got." He scrolled through the messages again. "The new information was added just after we headed away from the wreckage. So, whoever sent it didn't have advance knowledge of our destination."

"Small mercy. And it just looks like they added the information, right? Not anything to do with following up on a response we missed?"

"Impossible to tell," Asher said. "The answers will need to wait until we find the culprit."

Pen wished she didn't need to rely on Asher to find the information from the messages. The only clear thing to her was the content. "Could it be some other code which looks like location, direction, and velocity?"

"Even if it is, someone is still broadcasting data that puts us in danger." Asher chewed his lip in thought. "I can't guarantee we've broken every code, but I've yet to encounter one that would alter the content into something other than gibberish."

"What if the code was designed to produce this result if someone had to use a program to read it?" She would not settle for the explanation they had. The idea someone would attract their destruction was so alien to Pen her mind kept sliding off the facts.

"Again, it's possible, but there would have been some flag on the results. And we still need to find whoever is sending these."

He was right. No matter what she came up with as a reason that this was not what it seemed, they still had to find out who was sending the data and why. Maybe she just couldn't accept it because the list of suspects contained all the people she knew and trusted.

"So, where are the messages coming from?" Pen held her breath.

"Our ship. From three different public terminals." Asher turned from the screen. "We can view the security cameras."

It might help identify the person who broke into my quarters.

Asher showed her the screen, three different views of the public terminals in question. The time stamps matched the messages sent. The same person at each. Hooded jacket too big for the body, dark pants, gloves, not even a glance up at the camera.

"The same as the person who broke into my quarters," Pen said. "Am I wrong to feel relieved we only have one culprit?"

"Don't get comfortable with that idea. This could be different people dressed the same." He pointed to the different features. "Average height, no indication of sex, can't tell if the clothes are disguising the build. No idea how old."

Pen sighed. "Look, we can't keep getting drawn into dead ends here. Let me check what security found."

She contacted McIlroy. "Sorry, lieutenant, nothing to report. Seems like whoever did it knew how we would investigate. If I didn't know better, I'd say they had experience."

Pen thanked her and disconnected. "We need to figure out some suspects and investigate them ourselves. If we can't find anything soon, we go to Whitnal and the captain with what we gathered."

"Who are your suspects?" Asher asked.

She'd been trying to answer that question from the minute she realized there was a problem. "The only person I can be sure isn't doing it is me."

"So, I'm on your list?" Asher sounded like he approved of her logic.

"Am I on yours?"

He shook his head. "You were, but no way anyone would take a hit to the head like you did to cover something up."

"You think the attack was related?" Could someone have gotten to Flor?

"We must assume everything is related." Asher closed his eyes to think. "Has anything else happened lately that might explain what's going on?"

"No." Pen wasn't going to bring in the extent of the teenage bullying. "So how do I know you aren't the culprit? That you aren't just stringing me along to keep me from finding out what the real problem is?"

"Alas, I have no convenient wound to use as proof. Do you really think it's me?"

If he had come to her at the beginning, Pen would distrust his help. But she'd gone to him. He'd been nothing but helpful. She couldn't think of one time when he seemed to be leading her astray. And he was too tall to be the person in the security video. "No. So that narrows things down to the rest of the ship. No; to the rest of the fleet."

"Actually, you would need access to fake the authorizations. So that eliminates ninety percent of the population."

"Whitnal," Pen said. She had eliminated him, but now he fit the criteria.

"The captain," Asher said. "Anyone on the communications team. Kalin? Loke? Jo?"

Not a chance, Pen thought. "Your friends on the spy team. They have ways around authorization."

"Can we eliminate them?" Asher typed the list of names. "Start at the top? Whitnal?"

"He seems like he's helping," Pen said. "I just don't trust him. I guess that's not enough to make him guilty."

Asher was looking through a calendar. "He was at official meetings for everything we can confirm."

"Would he have a minion?" Was that Royce?

"If it is Roger, I would be his minion. How about the captain?"

"Why? He's spent his life keeping us safe."

"That's about to change. But until we know why someone is sending the transmissions, we can't understand his motive. And it's as farfetched as Roger."

"Not quite, but then who?"

"Kalin? Of all the people on the list, he has the most reason to sabotage us."

"No!"

"Hear me out, Pen. He might seem like he was devastated by being abandoned, but he was indoctrinated from birth to hate us. With his entire people gone, he just might be lashing out, or he could be completing his mission."

"Asher, he's the least likely. He has no access to anything. Me, Jo, and Loke are his only friends. We don't have the access. It's not him. If he wanted us dead, he'd do it directly." But he had known about her injury. "And before you start. Jo can't access this stuff either."

"He might have new security levels with his training."

She sighed out her frustration at the exercise. "Are you seriously thinking Jo would put us in danger?"

"No, but Loke?" Asher asked. "He is a leader. I'm not sure where that puts him in the hierarchy. But he might have access."

Her gut said no, but it was easy to check. "How do civilians get access to different authority levels?"

"Same way you do, we get a minimum and anything more must go through the communications transmission security office. We send a request and the day shift responds."

Gary and Chris? "So, someone like Loke needs to get his higher level of access approved?"

"Yeah. Civilian leaders change, so there's a process. A role like teacher gets slightly higher access with the job, but everything else has to be approved."

"Ranks get specific levels, too. Rarely anything more." Except Gary had just authorized her without question.

"I can find out," Pen said. "That means only a couple of people on the list."

She didn't like the fact Loke's name was there, but he fit the image on screen. All her friends did.

32

With nothing else to do until morning, Asher told Pen to get some sleep. She knew it was the right thing, but fear that the broadcast would attract the wrong attention while they waited kept her alert. Guilt about not informing the captain amplified her jitters. As soon as she was sure Gary and Chris were on duty, Pen donned her uniform, arranged her hair to cover the evidence of her head wound, and headed for the transmission security room.

"What do you want?" Chris asked as she walked into the room. "Gary isn't here and I'm too busy to chat."

This would be fast, Pen thought. "Where is he?" Maybe he was plotting the destruction of the fleet?

"Meeting with the boss. Looks like he might have found something interesting."

So, his attitude wasn't about her, Chris was just a bad loser. "Anything I should hear about?"

"If he's right, there's a gambling operation running ship to ship. Should you know about that?"

At least he hasn't stumbled on the broadcasts. "I'll get the full story from the captain, I'm sure. I need to ask you something. I'll be quick."

"Go ahead." He turned back to the screens.

"How do people get extra access to systems? I know you guys do the work, but it must need someone high up to sign off."

"Yes. Why do you want to know?"

She had to head off any curiosity, otherwise one of them would go rooting around for tidbits. "I'm starting to interview some of the newcomers. If they are unhappy with the access people have, I want to point them in the right direction."

"They all know who to talk to," Chris said. "We had a few of the new kids come to us. So, we made sure they got the message."

"Why were the kids asking?"

"Missing friends and wanted more access to talk. Kids don't think through the whole thing, right?"

"No. Can't have them bogging down the system." Pen figured she could guess who had asked. "So, have you given any extra access at all?"

"Not to them. It's not worth my career. Little snots thought they could bribe us." He laughed. "No idea why they thought it would work. Things must be different where they came from."

"As you said, they don't think things through. So did someone get access?"

"You, but that was on the captain's orders. Gary could have done it before you asked, but he wanted you to come to us."

"Glad I did. Anyone else?" Why was he avoiding the question?

"A couple of the new experts. They said they needed higher access, that they had it before. Captain signed off."

"Can you tell me who? If they are important enough to warrant special treatment, they will be great interview subjects."

He looked at her as if deciding whether she was testing him. Then he flicked his glance back at the screen. "Two of them. A guy named Brian Cook and a doctor, name of Tibel. I need to get back to my work."

Pen headed to her desk. A quick search revealed that the doctor worked with the biology team assessing the process for releasing their seeds. Also, she stood about two meters tall. Not their suspect. The other one was Jarl's dad.

Was he behind the bullying? It would make more sense if he was the culprit; distracting the public face of the leaders with petty issues would keep her from looking at him. But why? Why would anyone?

The only way to find answers was to meet with him. Pen sent a request to his pad and kept looking into him. A single father. Expert in long range communications. He'd been brought, along with his daughter, to work on the feeds from the scouts. Their job was to gather as much information about the planets as soon as possible. His specific duties focused on enhancing the range capabilities. He had every-thing needed to hack authorization codes and send a broad-cast. But why? Why? That was the constant question in her life.

Pen's pad pinged: Asher. Not a message. Pen glanced around before answering the call. She was alone in the room. "What did you find?"

"My background checks clear almost everyone except for Loke, who doesn't seem to have any skeletons we don't know about, and two of your communications team members. I need more information. Personnel files."

What could be in the files to clear or condemn anyone? "What about the new experts?" she asked, buying time before she agreed to violate the privacy of people she thought innocent.

"Not much information."

Pen told him what she'd found. "This feels like a good lead."

"They would have been vetted, Pen." Asher looked down, then nodded and faced the camera. "But maybe not enough. Their files might be here by now."

"What can you learn by looking at them?"

"You know what's in there. Psychological assessments, associations, incidents."

That was the reason she didn't want him to access them. "Loke's won't be there. Their records were destroyed with the ship."

"Not long ones, but they have all been through a counselor. Their histories recorded. Not everything we need, but better than what we have."

It will clear them, she hoped. "I can't access them without a lot of paperwork, or approval from the captain, but give me a bit of time to think of a way in."

"I know it's hard, Pen. But we need to set a trap. We must get our answers today. Those files will give us the tools."

"I said I would get them. Let's meet in the theater in a couple of hours."

"We're close, Pen. We know what we're looking for, we just need to dig a little more."

She knew that. But she also knew they needed help. And Asher would argue. A couple of hours would give her time to figure something out. More people meant a stronger trap and less danger.

"Yeah. See you at the theater." She signed off and closed her terminal. Janice had just come in and the unit was no longer a safe place to work.

She sent two messages and accepted the timing of the meeting from Jarl's father. Things were moving fast. Asher was right, she could feel the end coming. She only hoped it didn't mean the end of the fleet.

33

Two hours later Pen faced off with Asher. Kalin and Jo stood at the door letting her take care of the fight like she'd asked them to.

"Pen, you should have told me," he said. "Help is great, but I don't like being surprised."

It wasn't the battle she expected, and Pen felt embarrassed that she'd assumed Asher would be angry. "They are both off the list, right?" she asked, somehow unable to stop fighting a non-existent battle.

"Yes. And I understand how Jo wouldn't want to just hand over what we asked for." He looked toward the door. "What does Kalin bring? You said he has no authority or access."

"He's the only person I know who has experience in a real fight. I hope there won't be violence, but we need to be prepared."

Asher beckoned them over. "What do you know about the situation?"

"Pen told us what you found, and what you need to

confirm your suspicions. I can access the files here. Be aware if anyone looks, they'll know I've poked around."

"I can hide your presence," Asher said. "I think whoever did this is confident they covered their tracks. No one is likely monitoring the files."

Jo held out his hand for Asher's terminal. "I only have this authority because of my training rotation," he said. "I don't know if anyone is monitoring me. So be quick." He typed his password into the terminal and Pen saw a list of files pop up.

Asher took back the terminal and typed a few keys. "I'll have copies in about thirty seconds. Then we can look to our heart's content."

"Asher, stop doing that." Pen stared at the screen, appalled. "We only need a few files. Now you can access everyone's."

"It takes too long to pick and choose. I'll delete and shred the directory." He smiled at her. "Now you know how it feels when someone goes ahead and does something without a heads up."

"Like I didn't know that already. It's your default setting." Pen swallowed her discomfort. Jo and Kalin needed to see her confidence in Asher, not her annoyance.

"Kalin, what can you do to help?" Asher asked. "I mean other than if we get into a physical fight?"

"Pen needs protection," Kalin said. "Under your watch she got her head bashed in."

"You don't need to follow me around, Kalin," Pen said. How was she going to interview Brian Cook with a bodyguard?

"I can also blend better than any of you." Kalin waved to encompass the other three. "You can't be recognized, Asher.

Apart from your role on the mission, you depend on not being noticed, right? Jo and Pen are too well known. I'm the only one of us who might not pose a threat. The poor stranger whose whole world got destroyed. You'd be surprised at how a little sympathy lowers someone's guard."

"Any experience?" Asher sounded interested.

"We were trained in all the arts of war. One of the things I don't miss is the feeling of being watched all the time by everyone. I can listen to conversations without anyone noticing and I'm trained on how to sift the normal grousing from dangerous talk."

"I don't know how much we need that now," Asher said, "but I may have an offer for you when we are done here. You are looking for a job, right?"

"Does that mean you are finally taking my no?" Pen looked at Jo to check how he took the words. Not having to repeat her refusal would be nice.

"I still think you would be a wonderful spy, but you have no interest, and as Kalin pointed out, you are far too public a figure to succeed now."

"Are we going to talk all day, or should we do something to find the dirt we need?" Jo asked.

Pen checked the time. "I have an hour. Then I'm inter-viewing one of our suspects."

"Not alone," Jo said.

"Yes. It's about my actual duty. I'll be safe."

"Brian Cook?" Asher asked. "Let's start with his file."

Two minutes of review left Pen no nearer certainty. "He looks clean."

"It could all be cover," Asher said. "The interview is likely to get you a better idea of his intentions. Have you met him?"

"Only his daughter. She's one of that little gang."

"Then be careful. Make sure you make an escape plan and don't let him get behind you or between you and the door." Asher turned back to the files. "Let's check the communications team in case we missed something."

There was only so much room around the terminal, and they'd edged her out. It wasn't worth pushing her way in, and Jo and Kalin had fresh eyes. Maybe they would notice something she couldn't. Not that she'd bonded with the communications team, but her instinct was that they were innocent. Her time would be better spent answering questions and preparing for her meeting. She still hadn't come up with a way to prove Mr. Cook's alliances.

"Pen, what do you know about Sunshine and Chen?" Kalin asked.

"I hardly talked to them. Both were kind of helpful. Is there something in the file?"

"No. It's like your guy. Too clean." He left the group around the terminal. "I think I'll see if I can bump into them and bask in some of the sympathy."

Asher looked up. "See if you can do that with the rest of the team."

Kalin nodded and left the theater.

"How much longer will you be?" Pen asked.

"Almost done. Loke's file was about what we suspected," Asher said. "Do you want another check at Cook's file?"

"No... but... How about his daughter? Anything pointing to a reason she's so angry? I mean still angry."

"She hasn't made her interview appointment yet," Jo said. "It's tomorrow. I guess that's not really a flag. There are only so many slots available."

"Okay." She stifled the urge to look at Mellie's file. If she pried, how could she lecture Asher on privacy?"

"We'll keep looking," Asher said. "Go get ready for the interview. I suggest not your uniform. It's too official and will set him on guard even if he's innocent."

"Jo, make sure he cleans the files from his terminal before you leave."

hat if Jarl is home?

W The thought burst through Pen's mind as she reached to press the contact on Brian Cook's door.

Even worse, what if the whole gang of them had heard about the meeting? Pen took a breath. She hadn't considered anything but a one-on-one interview. It was too late to cancel, and they needed to be sure he wasn't part of the plans. If the girls were there, it was his problem, Pen decided. She was professional.

The door opened almost as soon as she pressed the chime.

"Pen, it's good to meet you in person." Brian Cook smiled warmly and held the door open for her. "Coffee?"

She watched as he worked in the kitchen. He fit the image on the video. Average height and build. His bright red hair would have been hidden by the hood. He walked with a slight limp. None of the videos recorded enough movement to notice. There was no tension in his stance; he came across as friendly and kind. Pen knew it had more to do with his smile and blue eyes than the fact he had coffee and cookies to offer. If he was planning the destruction of the fleet, would he be able to put such an open face to the world? Pen felt herself wanting to like him. A perfect skill for the culprit.

He joined her at the table and slid the plate of cookies toward her along with her cup of coffee. "Before we start, I need to get something off my chest."

"Go ahead. This is going to be informal anyway. I'll make a few notes, but that's it. You'll be asked to sign off on anything we publish with your name."

"Good to know. I want to apologize to you. My daughter's behavior had been less than stellar."

"You don't need to do that," Pen said, surprised by his words. "She's acting out a bit. I can understand how difficult it could be for her to leave her friends behind."

"Kind of you to say." He looked into his cup as though an answer floated on top. "It's not about coming here. She's been a challenge since her mother died."

Pen found herself sympathetic despite her suspicions. "I'm sure she'll settle. She found some friends, after all."

"Yes. I'm not crazy about them either, but what dad is? She didn't exactly run with the best people back home." He gave a chuckle. "Anyway. I do feel bad she pushed her friend to get your address. It will not happen again."

So, it wasn't Mellie. Who exactly ran the gang?

"Apology accepted." Pen wanted to move the conversation to more useful topics. "How has it been for you coming aboard? Jarl isn't the only one who left everything behind."

"Different for me," he said. "The work is here. I have a chance to be part of finding our new home. How could anything compare with that?"

This man was either the best actor she'd met, or exactly

what he seemed. "Exciting. I understand your work is pretty classified. How does it affect your home life?"

"I try to keep a balance, but Jarl's a teenager. Her schedule rarely intersects with mine." He sighed. "That sounded like an excuse. And maybe I am too involved in my work to handle her. Raising a teenager is all new to me. Her mother passed six months ago. I haven't quite gotten a handle on what she needs."

Maybe she would have been better off not coming here. The thought took Pen by surprise. It did explain Jarl's acting out more than just trying to fit in with a new group of friends. "I'm sure the counselor will give her some coping skills when she meets with her." As soon as the words were out, Pen realized she shouldn't know any of that information.

He looked up. "Jarl told me she had done her meeting."

Brian Cook had no idea what her security clearance was. That or he didn't care. "I was led to believe she is one of the few people who are scheduled for appointments tomorrow," Pen said.

He sighed. "This is harder than manipulating code to extend the capabilities of small scout ships. At least with them I'm sure when I'm making progress."

Pen crossed his name off the list of suspects. He was too interested in the future to want it destroyed. "I shouldn't tell you this, Mr. Cook, but I think you need to know. Jarl's appointment is at ten tomorrow morning with counselor Quan. She won't let you join the session, but you can escort Jarl to the door."

"I'll make the time. Thank you. I won't tell anyone." He sat straighter. "Now, what else would you like to ask me?"

Pen filled the time with innocuous questions and ended the interview.

As soon as she was in the corridor, she sent Asher a message. *Not him.*

Her head hurt again, and she needed some solitude. She'd wait for updates in her quarters.

35

Her pad pinged. Pen sat up and grabbed it. A light nap had eased her headache and she was ready to go. The message came from Asher. *Meet me in the equipment room where you were attacked. I have an idea.*

She was expecting an update from Kalin's activities. Or whatever they'd found in the files. But maybe he would do that when she saw him. If he'd found something that proved who attacked her, she could hand over that part of her problems to McIlroy. Anything to let her concentrate on the investigation would be welcome.

There was nothing from the captain about her plan, nor from Whitnal. She'd been asleep for an hour, still early enough to make progress after meeting Asher.

Pen changed into more casual clothes, as her interview civvies were a little too nice to wear in the dust and cobwebbed part of the ship.

It took thirty minutes before she could slip through the door. Today, finally, people wanted to talk to her. She had a pad full of notes and ideas; at least she'd be busy when this problem was solved.

She patted her pocket as she strode down the first passageway. The flashlight was heavy, but she needed to be sure. She wouldn't be caught in the dark again. When she turned the corner into the less familiar territory, Pen's body went on alert, remembering every pain and fear that she carried the last time she ventured this way. Asher better have a real clue.

Someone had sent maintenance mechs in this direction in the last day. The webs were gone, and the dust layer was scraped off. It couldn't have anything to do with her attack. Only two other people knew, and they wouldn't care about the state of this section. The facilities team must have plans. This wouldn't be a good place to hide out much longer.

The door to the equipment room was open.

Pen came to a stop. She needed to put her hand against the wall to steady herself. The anxiety from a few minutes ago had become full blown panic. It was hard to catch her breath, she felt cold and dizzy. Even knowing Asher waited for her didn't loosen its grip. She couldn't get enough air to call out to him.

Someone moved inside the room. Footsteps coming closer. More than one set. Pen forced in a lungful of air and tried to tell her brain she wasn't in danger. It didn't listen.

The footsteps moved away. Pacing. Asher was getting impatient. Another deep breath and the terror drained. Two more and she was able to take a step forward. And then another.

She stepped through the open door, still not quite able to call out. Pen pulled the flashlight out, hoping its heft would make her feel safer. *This is stupid. There is no threat.*

Someone touched her shoulder. Pen spun around but the person moved too quickly. Not Asher. Her instinct was right. This was a trap.

She heard a hiss and felt a sting on her hand.

Her knees gave way.

She tried to see who attacked her, but they turned off the lights as they approached. She tried to swing the flashlight, but her arm went dead.

Her eyes closed and she couldn't open them.

Then everything disappeared.

36

"Wake up."

Pen heard the voice but couldn't quite obey. Her eyelids were too heavy to force open.

"We didn't give you that much," the voice came again, petulant and bossy.

Pen licked her dry lips and tried again to open her eyes, no luck. She could feel bindings on her hands again, the existing wounds burning at new abrasions. She could hear the hum of the life support and each breath had a dryness that caught in the back of her throat.

Someone poked her shoulder. "I said wake up. We have work for you to do."

She knew the voice but couldn't dredge up a face or a name. This time her eyelids fluttered, but then closed.

"Are you sure about the dosage?" Another familiar voice.

"Yeah. Maybe we should have given her a bit less because we hit her head." That made three people.

Pen was sitting on some kind of hard chair. She kept her

eyes closed even though she was pretty sure she could open them. If they kept talking about her, maybe they'd slip, and she'd get a bit of information.

"She's faking." A sharp jab to Pen's ribs followed the words. "Open your eyes."

So much for subterfuge. Pen flicked her eyes open. Her captors were arranged around her, Mellie's face was close. Pen jerked, trying to head butt the girl. She moved out of range.

"Surprised?" Mellie asked. "I bet you are."

"Why?" Pen's voice was cracked. How long had they held her? "Can I have some water?"

"It's the drug," Jarl said. She held a bottle of water to Pen's lips and let her drink. "We need you sounding healthy."

Pen pulled away, water slopping onto her jacket. If it was the drug, she hadn't been missing long enough for anyone to worry. Surely if anyone had noticed, Asher would send teams combing the abandoned area. And that was where they held her. The taste of dust, the empty room. The lack of background noise. No other place on the ship would feel like this.

This time her bonds were tight, and with four girls watching, she wouldn't be able to wiggle free. Her best option was to stall long enough for an alert to go out. If she was good at it, she could get them to tell her why they were doing this.

Flor was a little to the side, Jarl and Mellie stood in front of Aila. Pen couldn't be sure who was the ringleader. She stared them down, waiting for someone to speak.

"Your counselors are much freer with the pharmaceuticals," Aila said. "A little sleeping serum can be turned easily into a stronger version, if you know your chemistry."

"Don't tell her that," Flor said. "We need a few secrets to parlay a deal when this is over."

Not expecting to get away with this. Good. It means they don't intend to kill me.

"It pays to have important parents," Jarl said. "They won't let us be locked up for long. The captain needs to learn he's not in charge anymore."

The captain needs to tell Whitnal to keep the civilians in line. They were still in space.

Mellie leaned in again, staying just outside Pen's reach. "You really want to know why?"

Pen threw up the water all over Mellie. "Sorry," she mumbled. "Head injury and drugs don't go well."

"You did that on purpose," Mellie screamed. She slapped Pen hard enough to rock the chair.

"Stop," Flor said, her voice dull. "We need her to speak."

"We aren't going to run away," Jarl said. "We are the generation who has to live with this decision. We'll be trapped on a planet when the enemy comes."

If they had any idea what combat was like, they would be pushing to get away faster.

"You saw the wreckage," Pen said. "How are we going to fight that in space?"

"Lies." Flor stepped closer. "It wasn't real. The captain just didn't want to fight. We need to bring the enemy to us and deal with the problem. We need to see the real feeds."

Pen heard the conviction in Flor's voice. They weren't going to be swayed with logic. "How will you know anything we show you is real?"

"We're not stupid," Flor said. "I can analyze data. You already know Jarl can make drugs. Aila and Mellie know how to convince people. We know it's going to be hard. But we are right."

"So, what's next then? Keeping me here won't get you any of that. Eventually someone will come looking. When they find me tied up, they won't listen to you. Assaulting an officer, unlawful confinement, let alone the drugs and the hacking. Why would anyone want to listen to your version?"

Flor smiled, slow and mean. "We've already figured that out. People will see us being dragged out in restraints. Maybe the military won't care, but we have friends. Our parents have power. Our plan will get out."

Pen doubted that anyone liked these four bullies. Their treatment of her wouldn't be isolated. But maybe they didn't know the difference between fear and like.

"She's stalling," Mellie said. "Tell her what to do."

Flor turned around to look at Mellie. "I decide when we move on. You just want to get out of those clothes. Well, get used to it. We are not rushing this."

So, Flor was in charge. Surprising, but the knowledge helped. Pen wasn't sure how she would use the information, but it was something.

"Why now?" Pen asked. "You've been sending messages for a while." *Keep them talking.*

"Maybe we want to send a stronger signal," Aila said. "Why should we tell you?"

Flor didn't completely control her friends. Pen could work with that. "A lot of maybes. Are you sure you know what you're doing?"

"Shut up, Aila." Flor indicated the others should move back. "Stop trying to divide us. We are not going to stop."

It was time to test how far Pen could push Flor before she lashed out. Find out how much she needed Pen in good shape to complete the plan. "How do you know this enemy can understand your message?"

"They don't need to. They can trace where it's coming

from." Flor tilted her head. "Why are you interested? What are you planning?"

"To be honest, I'm trying to figure out how much of a real threat your actions create. If you haven't thought through all the possibilities, this is just a stupid kid's game."

"We are not kids." Flor's eyes narrowed to slits. She did not like to be challenged.

"It looks to me like you are two-year-olds having a temper tantrum." No reaction from Flor. "I mean what kind of person wants to destroy everything? Isn't there someone you love enough to want them to live?"

"You don't know me," Flor said, her temper heating up. "This isn't about destroying anything. It's about having a future. It's about exposing the lies."

"A lot of reasons, but you are ignoring the big one." Pen braced herself. "The images you saw from the wreckage were real. We have no way of fighting that. On a planet, we might be able to build a defense, but in space there's nowhere to hide."

"That's all a lie," Flor said. The other three mumbled something in agreement.

Pen ignored them. Flor was the one she needed to break. "Who told you that? You couldn't have come up with it on your own."

"Why not? Do you think we are so easy to manipulate? That some adult has to trick us into believing something?"

"Yes. And that someone is putting you on the line. You'll get caught. The whole fleet will know the danger you created. You'll be in the brig because it will be the only place we can keep you alive."

"No. We'll broadcast the real images. Then people will know."

Pen laughed in Flor's face. "You'll be pushed out an airlock before you get a chance."

The other girls were looking worried. Flor must have sensed the change because she turned from Pen to look at them.

"What are you doing cowering in the corner? You know I'm right."

Mellie stepped in front of the others. "Pen makes some good points. But we don't know what you are waiting for. We don't need to listen to her points. We can't turn back."

Why not? Pen caught her breath. That sounded very final.

"We don't need to turn back." Flor sounded puzzled. "I want her to know why. I want people like her to know we aren't going to just sit around and let them plan our future without us."

"You won't live to enjoy a future," Pen said.

"You think what you planned is a good future? You grew up on the ship with all the tech and safety. So did we. You think digging around on a planet is going to be fun? We'll starve half the time. We'll die of some kind of disease, or predator."

Selfish little bitch. "So you'll need to work hard. It will get easier for your kids, and their kids. That's what a future is about. The ships won't last forever, Flor. Someone in the future might have to choose less habitable planets to colonize."

"Yeah. I've been given the lecture. My future is important too," she screamed the last words.

"Flor, tell her," Aila said. "Stop fighting and tell her. We need to take the next step. You can beat her into submission afterward."

It took Flor minutes to calm down enough to do more than stand rigid with fury.

"Yes. It's time." She turned back to Pen. "We've received an answer."

37

P en struggled against the restraints. She needed to get out. How long did they have?

"Settle down," Flor said. "You are going to call the captain and tell him to come to us."

"No." Pen choked out the word. She had no choice but to stop trying to free herself. Her body was too damaged to put up a real fight. Head injury, lack of sleep, stress, and a dose of drugs that probably interacted badly with her painkillers left her with no reserves to keep going. "Bringing him here won't help."

"He has this silly habit of strolling around without protection. Bring him here so we can talk to him."

Why would he need protection?

Pen was having difficulty following the girl's logic. She relaxed and took in a few gasps of air. Focus on only one thing.

"Good. Now we have this." Flor held Pen's pad out. "So he'll take the call, right?"

"My hands are tied. How am I going to make the call?"

"I'll hold it. Just look at the screen so it will unlock." Flor nudged Pen's chin up. "There."

"He won't just come," Pen said. Her mind was racing, trying to figure out how to warn the captain, wishing she'd told him what was going on.

"Your contacts are only numbers." Flor tilted her head. "The captain is the most important person you know. So, he must be number one?"

Pen had set her pad to order her contacts by the most frequent calls. Asher would answer if she called the first one. "Fine, I'll call. Where am I?"

"Next door to the equipment room," Flor said. "You remember enough to direct him?"

Pen nodded and endured a wave of nausea. "Okay."

"We'll be listening. Don't try to trick us."

"If you put the call on speaker setting, he'll know something's wrong. He'll send security forces ahead."

"Liar," Flor shouted.

"No, Flor," Jarl said. "She's right. It's okay. We'll hear her side. She can't trick us."

Pen watched Jarl as she spoke. It was impossible to tell if she'd had a change of heart. It didn't matter, her words helped Pen.

Flor pressed the connect icon and held the phone to Pen's ear. She'd be able to hear if someone spoke, but hopefully not that it wasn't the captain.

"Pen?"

"Captain." Pen couldn't let him say anything that would give her away. "I need to show you something in the abandoned sector."

There was a pause, then Asher spoke, "Is it critical?"

"Yes, sir. Highly critical."

"Where?"

Pen gave the instructions, wishing she could tell him to bring weapons. "Can you come now?"

"Lieutenant Tromarin, I have priorities. Can this wait for an hour?"

Nicely done. The captain would not come on her request. She looked at Flor. There was no way to ask for time. And Pen didn't see her being cooperative. "It would be better to get this done right away, sir."

Another pause. "Fifteen minutes, lieutenant, and this better be good."

Asher ended the call.

"Good little girl." Flor punched Pen in face.

She was only out for a few minutes this time. The first sound that came to her was bickering. She kept her eyes closed, hoping to hear a crack in the loyalty.

"You didn't have to do that," Jarl said. "She looks bad. He'll know as soon as he sees her."

Someone got slapped.

"I know what I'm doing," Flor said. "Let him see her. It will be too late to escape. And he'll learn how serious we are."

"Flor," Mellie's voice. "You can't face the captain like this. He won't listen."

"Don't hit her!" That was Aila. "If you keep hitting us, I'm walking out. If you can't get control, you'll ruin everything."

"She's right," Mellie said. "Flor, we're a team. We're on your side."

The panting must be coming from Flor. Pen cracked open her eyes. They were clustered in the corner, not paying attention to her. She still couldn't get free, but she could stir the pot. Keeping Flor out of control would help Asher.

"She treats you like that, and you still want to be tied to her?"

Mellie turned at Pen's words. "You did this to her. Flor would never hurt us if you hadn't pushed her."

"I don't think that's true. Look at Aila. She's not buying it. I'm guessing she's been the recipient of Flor's anger before."

"Aila?" Mellie asked.

"She's lying." Aila didn't sound convincing.

"I'm not," Pen said. *How long had she been out? Was Asher outside the door?*

"Ignore her," Jarl said. Her cheek bloomed bright red where Flor's hand had made contact. "Flor, pull your shit together. The captain will be here in a couple of minutes."

"Drag her out of sight. I want him to see me when he comes in." Flor smoothed her hair and moved to the center of the room.

Her mood changed too fast. Flor must have been fooling her counselor for a while. She needed help.

38

"If you make this much noise, the captain will not just walk in," Pen said. It would be great for the girls to be distracted but Pen worried that things would get too far out of control. Her rescue would come too late.

"She's right, Flor," Mellie said. "We need to be cool when he gets here. He won't listen if we're freaking out."

"I will be fine. Do as I said. In fact, make sure she can see what happens. I want her to understand how the future will look." She strode to Pen. "Check her bindings. She's too confident."

Jarl and Aila dragged Pen into the corner. Pen faced the room but wouldn't be seen until everyone was inside.

"Gag her." Flor moved to stand in the center of the room, facing the door.

Mellie smirked. "Use this." She took off her vomit covered teeshirt and handed it to Jarl.

At least it's my puke. Pen forced herself not to fight the gag. They had to think she was complying. It wouldn't take much to render her unconscious again. And another hit to her head was likely to cause more permanent damage than a headache.

Everything went silent.

"Five minutes," Flor said.

Footsteps sounded outside. Only one person. Asher better have a weapon.

The door opened. Asher stepped in. "You will release Lieutenant Tromarin and come with me."

"Who are you? Where's the captain?" Flor was losing control again.

"He isn't coming. One more chance."

"Get him here or we will kill her."

Flor's words didn't have the effect she expected.

Asher smiled. Her gang shuffled away. Apparently, there were lines they wouldn't cross. Although if they had attracted the enemy, it was just a matter of time. Everyone would be dead soon.

Suddenly the situation changed. Kalin and Jo came into the room, weapons raised. Asher took a step toward Flor, pulling a stun-and-disable weapon. She was relieved; despite what they'd done, Pen wanted the girls to survive.

She tried to spit out the gag, but it didn't move. Asher needed to know the enemy had responded. Taking these girls fast was important.

"I said he's not coming. How do we do this? You come quietly and we finish this in a civilized manner, or you make us use force. You'll come either way."

"We can kill her faster than you can stop us."

"True, but she knows the risks of her job. We'll be sad, but you won't stop us. And we don't need all of you."

Kalin and Jo shifted their aim. Now all the weapons were aimed at Flor. She was shaking with rage. Pen wasn't sure she'd have lasted under the pressure of two trained killers aiming large weapons at her head.

"We can still do it," Mellie said. "Flor, it doesn't need to be here. They can't hide us away. People will see us being taken through the corridors. They will ask questions. My dad will step in."

"Your father is waiting for you," Asher said. "All of your parents are aware of your actions. They will not interfere. They will be questioned about what they knew."

Pen watched, hoping Flor would see sense.

Everything seemed to happen at once.

Flor pulled a weapon out of her pocket and aimed at Asher.

Asher took the hit, spinning around from the force.

Kalin and Jo fired.

Flor dropped to the ground.

The three girls screamed.

Asher bent and put restraints around Flor's limbs.

Kalin and Jo changed their aim to the cluster of very frightened girls.

Asher pulled out Pen's gag and released her binding.

She nodded to the wound on his arm, blood flowed down his shirt. "Are you okay?"

"It will be fine. You?"

"I could use a toothbrush." She rose from the chair and went to check Flor. She was unconscious but not wounded.

"You can't tell what setting these things are on," Jo said. "You didn't think we'd kill some kids, did you?"

"If you knew what they did..."

"Sent a broadcast out to attract a fleet-killing enemy?" Kalin asked.

"I told them," Asher said, "and the captain, and Whitnal."

"How did you know it was them?" Pen didn't look at the prisoners. They were no longer the priority.

"We didn't exactly," Jo said. "But you were in trouble. And it would be a huge coincidence if that had nothing to do with this message."

"They got a reply," Pen said. "We have to do something."

"We know about the reply," Asher said. "You need medical help. We can deal with it from here."

"No! I'm not going to miss the end. I'll get fixed up enough to join you. Where are you taking them?"

Kalin walked to the door. "All clear."

Asher's medic friend walked in with her equipment. "I suggested you take it easy, lieutenant. This is the opposite."

She checked the captives and declared them safe to move. Pen got a scan and a painkiller and a mint. "You will report to medical within the next two hours or I'm coming to drag you there."

39

The briefing room was full. The captain, Whitnal and Loke were at the head of the room. The girls were restrained across the room. Around the oval table sat their parents, Jo, Asher, and Kalin with Pen in the middle.

She gripped the arm of her chair to hide the tremor in her fingers. As soon as the meeting ended and they had plans in place for evading annihilation, she was going to give herself over to the medics. It would be nice to rest for a few decades.

"This is an unusual situation." The captain looked around the table. "Usually when someone has committed a crime, I would not be involved. Your actions, ladies, mean we need to tread carefully. Mr. Whitnal and Mr. Ortiz are here to represent the two civilian populations aboard, your parents to witness what is about to happen. And these others are here because I believe they deserve to see the outcome of their investigation."

The captain gave Pen a look that promised a hard

conversation later. Pen hoped to be put in a medical coma for a while to avoid explaining the secrecy.

The girls had lost all the bravado. Flor didn't raise her eyes from the carpet. Jarl had been crying and didn't seem to be finished. Mellie and Aila both kept looking at their parents, seeming shocked that they didn't speak.

"You put the entire fleet at risk," the captain continued. "I understand you believe we altered the feeds from the wreckage to manipulate our populations. You are half correct. The data was altered."

"I told you!" Flor shouted, suddenly animated.

"Not for the reason you think. We are going to show you the raw data. I warn you that the parts we deleted are horrifying." The captain turned to Kalin. "If you wish to leave until this part is over, Kalin, we all understand."

"I do not."

Why is he putting himself through this? If the captain was warning them, it would not be easy to watch.

"I've seen it before, Pen," he muttered, then kept his eyes on the table.

"Play the raw feeds," the captain said to someone not in the room.

The wreckage gave enough points of reference to show how the scouts wove through space. Pen squeezed the chair arm harder as her vertigo returned but couldn't look away.

"*Dark Prospect,* this needs to be seen by someone before you stream." The scout's voice was strained. "Fuck!"

A piece of debris swung across the sensors. An arm, ripped from a suit, the shoulder a mass of frozen blood.

Then the screen went red.

"Sorry *Dark Prospect*, blood crystal field. Should clear soon."

Another scout took lead. Pieces of ship slid past the sensor, pushed away by the shields. The scout banked as a large piece of the drive was revealed behind a screen of microscopic debris.

The feed blinked to another ship and they saw the cluster of bodies looking like empty survival suits. But instead of what the rest of the ship had seen, Pen stared at blood and body pieces. Somehow, seeing an eye and finger float by was worse than an arm. All of the fragments looked like they'd been tossed there after the major destruction.

"They weren't killed quickly," Pen said. "Someone took those parts first."

She looked away from the screen to the people in the room. Kalin was staring at his hands. Only the girls were still watching the screen, and none of them seemed to disbelieve the reality.

"Stop the feed," the captain said. "So, you thought we should deal with this threat now?" he asked the girls.

"Why didn't you show that at first?" Flor asked. "We were right that you changed it. What else did you lie about?"

"What do you think would have happened if everyone had seen that?" Whitnal asked. "Panic. The captain and I decided that the reality of a new enemy was enough."

"We got a reply," Mellie said quickly. "It's too late. I mean, I'm sorry that we did it. But it's too late."

Pen pressed her lips together to avoid saying anything because even with everything they did, she wanted to comfort them. She was here to witness, not excuse.

"Well, what do you think we should do now?" the captain asked. "You obviously thought we could win a fight even with what we let you see."

"We need to run," Jarl said. "Change direction. I can turn off the broadcast. We'll find another planetary system somewhere. We have to turn away from this course."

"There are no other planetary systems in the database near this sector. We will spend lifetimes finding other potentials."

"So, we're just going to wait for death?" Mellie stared at her father. "Do something, Dad."

"There is nothing I can do. Mellie, I love you and I'll stand by you, but I can't support your behavior. You did not learn this from me or your mother."

Whitnal held up a hand to stop the response. Pen was glad; she didn't need another bout of Mellie's temper.

"Mr. Jones," he said to Asher, "I think it's time for you to report."

Asher stood. "Once we knew who was responsible, it was easy to track the origin of the signal. We found your broadcast and it is shut down."

"But she told you, we got a reply. It doesn't matter." Jarl struggled with her restraints like she could break free and outrun the danger.

"Don't worry, you haven't killed everyone. I sent the response." Asher looked at Pen. "You said something a few days ago that got me thinking. We couldn't trace the messages back, but we could reply. I tried to let you know, but I think you were resting. It flushed them out. I didn't anticipate that it would put you in danger."

Pen almost passed out in relief. "You could have told me before now," she said.

"I tried, but Sheila wouldn't let me near you."

"I believe you will take custody of the four criminals," Whitnal said to Asher.

"Yes, security personnel are waiting outside."

Loke opened the door and four officers entered, took possession of one girl each and marched them from the room. None of the parents protested.

"What's going to happen to them?" Pen asked.

"They will be fine, Pen," the captain said. He turned to the parents. "You will be able to speak to them in an hour. We cannot let them out of custody."

Jarl's dad stood. "Thank you, captain. I agree they will be safer in official hands. If what they did gets out, I'm afraid that they will not live long."

40

The medical coma was not an option. The doctors scanned every part of her and declared her fit for light duty. Since her assignment was actually communication, it meant she went back to her usual duties. A night's sleep and a long shower gave Pen a feeling of health. She knew it wouldn't last, but the alternative of lying in bed wasn't attractive after being so deep in the action.

She pulled on her uniform and dragged her hair back to cover the wound.

Lieutenant Tromarin, report to the captain's quarters. Her private comm stated the order in a neutral voice.

Time to find out if I've screwed my career.

When she arrived, Wes Royce was with the captain. No Whitnal, so at least she didn't need to face being dressed down in front of a civilian.

"Lieutenant, I want a full report of your activities over the last four days. No more secrets."

Pen glanced at Royce. He firmed his lips, threatening her to silence. Pen could take the captain's words literally and Royce would be dumped in it, but then he'd just be worse. "I apologize for the lack of disclosure, sir. I have no excuse for withholding information."

"No, you don't. But I assume you have reasons. Royce will take notes. I want this all on the record now. In the future, when you do something like this again, I'll have ammunition."

He knew her too well. Pen didn't bother to argue that she'd never take such risks again.

"It came to my attention that we had a situation with our communications security. I sought out Asher Jones for assistance in finding sufficient evidence for you to act on my suspicion. I worked with Asher to investigate what appeared to be a serious breach of fleet security. During that time, my quarters were broken into, I received a head wound, and some serious resistance about my authority levels from people who should have been helping.

"In hindsight, I should have suspected the girls earlier. They were aggressive toward me for no apparent reason."

"Your reason for not giving me a heads up?" The captain didn't plan to let her off the hook.

Pen explained her need to find proof first, added the last few details about her attack and then stood, waiting for punishment.

"Thank you. Royce, you are dismissed. Please send in our guests."

The guests turned out to be Whitnal and Loke.

"You did a good job, Pen." the captain said. "I hope in the future you don't take too much on yourself. We are here to help."

"Not just us," Whitnal said. "Loke and I, of course, represent the two civilian groups. We've been in discussion with the other captains and what civilian leaders there are."

Was she about to be sent off ship?

"You look like you expect punishment, Pen." Loke laughed. "I guess, maybe this feels like one to you."

"Please tell me," Pen said. "I've been beaten and drugged. I'm not sure I can take any more suspense."

"You are no longer assigned as the ship's communications officer." The captain looked at Whitnal, who nodded for him to continue. "You will liaise with the entire fleet and advise on sundry issues that may affect our ability to become a united colony."

Pen couldn't absorb the words. "But I did a lousy job."

"You saved the fleet, Pen," Loke said. "And we learned something. You heard the sundry issues part, right? You decide what needs to be done."

"But I'm a lieutenant. How will I get people on other ships to listen to me?"

"I thought of that, Lieutenant Commander Tromarin."

They looked at her as if she was crazy for questioning the job. Well, maybe she was wrong. "Aye, sir."

WANT MORE?

Will the last of humanity find a home or be destroyed by the mysterious alien ship? Use the QR code to grab your copy of ATTACK today!

If you enjoyed reading FLIGHT, please consider helping other readers to find the story by leaving a review.

FREE EBOOK

Claim your copy of Running the Game when you use the QR code below to sign up for my newsletter and cheer on Pen as she vies for a commission in the military.

ALSO BY PA WILSON

For more books by P A Wilson

Use the QR code below or go to pawilson.ca

ABOUT THE AUTHOR

Perry Wilson is a Canadian author based in Vancouver, BC who has big ideas and an itch to tell stories. Having spent some time on university, a career, and life in general, she returned to writing in 2008 and hasn't looked back since (well, maybe a little, but only while parallel parking).

She is a member of the Vancouver Writers Social Group, The Royal City Literary Arts Society, and The Surrey Writing Workshop. Perry has self-published several novels. She writes the Madeline Journeys, a fantasy series about a high-powered lawyer who finds herself trapped in a magical world, the Quinn Larson Quests, which follows the adventures of a wizard named Quinn who must contend with volatile fae in the heart of Vancouver, and the Charity Deacon Investigations, a mystery thriller series about a private eye who tends to fall into serious trouble with her cases, and The Riverton Romances, a series based in a small town in Oregon, one of her favorite states. Her stand-alone novels are Breaking the Bonds, Closing the Circle, and The Dragon at The Edge of The Map.

For more information
www.pawilson.ca
pawilson@pawilson.ca

ACKNOWLEDGMENTS

People think that the process of writing is solitary. That's not the case for me. I have help from so many people it would be hard to acknowledge everyone, but I'll give it a try.

The support and inspiration I get from my writer's groups is incalculable. The Vancouver Writers Social Group opens my mind to other ways of telling a story. The Royal City Literary Arts Society gives me the opportunity to meet and share with other writers who have more knowledge than I do. The Other 11 Months group is where I learn about getting the words on the page. And my critique group who helps me find the best parts of the story I want to tell. Thanks to all of the members of these great groups.

Last of all, but definitely a huge part of the process, my beta readers. These are the people who love stories and are willing, and more than able, to tell me if my finished story is ready for you, my readers.

www.ingramcontent.com/pod-product-compliance
Lightning Source LLC
Chambersburg PA
CBHW020600180626
46810CB00007B/2583